W9-BLK-624

WITHDRAWN

LARGE PRINT ED.

*Also by Nancy Atherton
in Large Print:*

Aunt Dimity Beats the Devil

Aunt Dimity
DETECTIVE

Aunt Dimity
DETECTIVE

NANCY ATHERTON

Thorndike Press • Waterville, Maine

Published in 2002 by arrangement with Viking Penguin, a member of Penguin Putnam Inc.

Thorndike Press Large Print Mystery Series.

The tree indicium is a trademark of Thorndike Press.

The text of this Large Print edition is unabridged.
Other aspects of the book may vary from the original edition.

Set in 16 pt. Plantin by Christina S. Huff.

Printed in the United States on permanent paper.

Library of Congress Cataloging-in-Publication Data

Atherton, Nancy.
    Aunt Dimity, detective / Nancy Atherton.
      p. cm.
    ISBN 0-7862-3843-7 (lg. print : hc : alk. paper)
    1. Dimity, Aunt (Fictitious character) — Fiction.
    2. Women detectives — England — Cotswold Hills —
Fiction.   3. Cotswold Hills (England) — Fiction.   4. Large
type books.   I. Title.
    PS3551.T426 A942 2002
    813'.54—dc21   2001054254

For
the people of Bellflower,
good neighbors all

Chapter
1

My family and I were three thousand miles away when the murder took place in Finch. We had what my lawyer husband called "a *nearly* airtight alibi." The fact that our twin sons weren't quite two years old made their involvement unlikely, but since I was — according to Bill — capable of arranging anything, anywhere, regardless of time and space, he was forced to consider me a suspect. I wasn't sure whether to be flattered or appalled by his boundless faith in me.

Bill and I were Americans, though we lived in England now, in a honey-colored cottage in the Cotswolds, near the small village of Finch. Finch was a somnolent hive of inactivity, a rural backwater awash with retirees and seasonal tides of vacationing city-dwellers. It was a quiet place where people led quiet lives, and it suited us to a T. Bill ran the European branch of his family's venerable law firm from an office on the square, while I stayed at home with Will and Rob and a reliable English nanny-in-residence. We simply couldn't imagine a better life.

We had family obligations on the far side of the Atlantic, however, and the first three months of the New Year had been spent fulfilling them. We stayed with Bill's father at the family mansion in Boston, where Bill's snooty aunts subjected us to a head-spinning whirl of social calls intended to introduce the twins to every stuffed shirt in the Boston Brahmin directory. I adored my father-in-law, but social whirling wasn't my cup of tea. By the end of the three months I was more than happy to return to the life I'd left behind in Finch.

I was standing in the living room the day after our return, enjoying the sight of an April shower bathing the hawthorne hedge, when the vicar's wife pulled into our graveled drive. I was pleased, as always, to see her. Lilian Bunting was a slender, scholarly woman, middle-aged, mild-mannered, and as shrewdly observant as a case-hardened cop. If anyone could fill me in on three months' worth of Finchocentric gossip, it would be Lilian.

I met her at the front door, took her umbrella, and offered to take her raincoat, but she resisted.

"I can't stay, Lori," she informed me. "I

really must get back to Teddy."

"Is the vicar sick?" I asked, with some concern.

"No, but he soon will be if this business isn't cleared up expeditiously." Lilian clasped her hands together worriedly. "That's why I'm here. I have a favor to ask of you. I would have asked it of Emma Harris, but she and Derek are spending a few days in Devon."

"So that's where they are." Emma Harris was my nearest neighbor and closest friend in England. I'd found a message from her on my answering machine when I'd come home, but when I'd tried to return her call, no one had answered.

"I didn't like to ask for such a favor over the telephone," Lilian was saying. "I wouldn't ask at all if it weren't for Teddy."

My concern increased. Lilian Bunting was a stickler for social niceties, yet she hadn't welcomed me home after my long absence or made the requisite inquiries about Bill and the boys. Her hair was mussed, her face drawn, and she seemed distracted, almost fretful.

I leaned forward. "What's wrong, Lilian?"

"It's Nicky," she said. "Nicholas Fox, my nephew. Nicky's a darling boy, but he's staying with us for a fortnight, and I don't know what to do with him. There's no one his age in the village, and as Teddy and I will be fully engaged tomorrow afternoon, I was wondering if I might . . ." She looked at me imploringly.

"Bring Nicky here," I said promptly. "The boys and I will find a way to keep him busy." As a mother of twins, I was accustomed to coping with a fair amount of chaos. The prospect of adding one more child to the mix didn't faze me in the least.

Lilian grasped my hand. "Thank you, Lori. I know how exhausted you must be after your long journey."

"I'm fit as a fiddle," I countered. "We took the Concorde, so jet lag isn't an issue. Bill felt so peppy that he decided to stay in London until Saturday, to catch up on paperwork."

"Excellent." Lilian smoothed her hair. "It will relieve my mind to leave Nicky with you while Teddy and I attend the inquest."

"Inquest?" I repeated.

"A waste of time," Lilian said firmly. "We already know when, where, and how the poor woman was murdered."

"Murdered?" I echoed, beginning to feel like a slightly addled parrot.

Lilian eyed me closely. "Good heavens," she said. "You haven't heard."

"What haven't I heard?" I asked.

"There's been a murder," said Lilian, "in Finch."

I was certain I'd misunderstood her. The words "murder" and "Finch" didn't belong in the same sentence unless "never happens" came in between. Finch was a rural haven, not an urban jungle. The last crime committed in the village had been the theft of a series of obscure pamphlets from the vicar's study. On a crime-spree scale from one to ten, pamphlet-pilfering didn't even register. Murder, on the other hand, was a calamity of seismic proportions.

"M-murder?" I faltered, adding inanely, "Are you sure?"

Lilian shrugged. "As sure as one can be. The police seem to think —"

"Who?" I interrupted. Familiar faces were flickering past my mind's eye with gut-wrenching speed. "Who was murdered?"

"Mrs. Hooper," Lilian answered.

"*Pruneface?*" I cried, then ducked my head to avoid Lilian's disapproving glare. "Sorry. That's what Mr. Barlow called her when he pointed her out to me on the square. He didn't seem particularly fond of her."

"Prunella Hooper may not have been universally admired," Lilian said stiffly, "but she was enormously helpful to Saint George's.

11

Her flower arrangements were second to none, and she was always eager to volunteer for the most menial of tasks. Teddy and I found her a welcome addition to the parish."

I nodded, suitably chastened. Prunella Hooper had moved to Finch just before Christmas, which explained why I knew so little about her. She'd rented Crabtree Cottage from Peggy Taxman, Finch's postmistress and the owner of the Emporium, the village's general store. Mrs. Hooper and I had never been formally introduced, but we'd exchanged pleasantries in passing. I remembered her as a short, plump woman in late middle age who wore too much makeup and curled her tinted hair in an out-of-date bouffant style.

"How was she killed?" I asked.

"She was hit on the head with the proverbial blunt instrument," Lilian answered. "It happened ten days ago, in her cottage. Peggy Taxman found her shortly after nine in the morning, lying in a pool of blood near the front-parlor window, where she keeps — *kept* — all of those flowers."

"The geraniums," I said, and wondered briefly who would tend the hanging plants that crowded every window in Crabtree Cottage.

Lilian's brow furrowed as the hall clock

struck the hour. "I'm sorry, Lori, but I must run. Mrs. Hooper's death has upset Teddy terribly. He's in no condition to entertain my nephew."

"Well, I am," I told her. "I'm looking forward to meeting Nicky, and the twins will enjoy having a new playmate."

Lilian pressed my hand gratefully, took up her umbrella, and plunged back into the pouring rain. I waited until her car had disappeared between the hedgerows, then headed for the solarium.

It was a blustery April day, windy, wet, and colder than it had any right to be, exactly the sort of day that made me thankful for the glass-paneled room that stretched across the back of the cottage, where my sons could enjoy a reasonable facsimile of fresh air without the attendant risk of pneumonia. Will and Rob were there now, under their nanny's watchful gaze, wholly absorbed in dismantling the fleet of toy trucks bestowed upon them in Boston by their adoring grandfather.

"Annelise," I said from the doorway, "do you have a minute?" When the young woman had joined me, I asked quietly if she knew that a murder had taken place in Finch.

"Of course I do," she replied. "Mum told me about it the day after it happened."

Annelise had come with us to Boston but had kept in close touch with her family by telephone.

"Why didn't you tell me and Bill?" I asked.

"Mum said it'd put a damper on your holiday, and besides, old Pruneface was no great loss. 'Good riddance to bad rubbish,' Mum says."

I stared at her, openmouthed. Annelise was one of the most compassionate young women on earth, and her mother was kindness itself. They were the last people I'd expect to speak so extremely ill of the dead.

"Aren't you being a little harsh?" I said.

"Not nearly so harsh as she deserved," Annelise retorted. "No one was sad to see her go except for the Buntings and Mrs. Taxman, and they didn't know the half of it."

"The half of what?" I asked.

"The mischief she got up to." Annelise folded her arms. "I'm sorry, but I can't say more. Mum ordered us not to dignify that woman's wicked rumors by repeating them."

It was an exercise in futility to countermand an order issued by the matriarch of the Scaiparelli clan, so I turned my attention to the less daunting task of preparing lunch.

★ ★ ★

Two hours later, I stood in the clearing atop Pouter's Hill, gazing through filmy gray curtains of rain without seeing much of anything.

Pouter's Hill rose steeply from the meadow beyond my back garden. Climbing it had become a homecoming ritual, a way of reacquainting myself with the countryside after a prolonged separation. More often than not, I found the view soothing — patchwork fields, ever-changing sky, sheep-speckled hills — but it brought me no peace of mind that day.

I couldn't stop thinking about the first time I'd seen Prunella Hooper, the day Mr. Barlow had pointed her out to me across the square. His comments had made such an impression on me that I could remember them verbatim.

"I've seen her type before," he'd said. "They simper to your face while they stab you in the back. Sneaky-mean, my dad used to call 'em, and he knew a thing or two, did my dad. Steer well clear of her, is my advice. Women like her make trouble wherever they go."

I couldn't help wondering if Mr. Barlow's words had been prophetic. Had Mrs. Hooper made trouble in Finch? Was that what

15

Annelise had meant when she referred to "wicked" rumors? Had one of the rumors been wicked enough to trigger the ultimate retribution?

Had a villager killed Pruneface Hooper?

It seemed highly unlikely. It would be daylight madness for a local to commit a murder in a small community where everyone knew who wanted to murder everyone else and how they would do it — and when and where and why — given the chance.

Yet someone had killed Prunella Hooper. Someone had clouted her on the head and left her to die beneath the vibrant array of potted geraniums hanging in the front-parlor window of Crabtree Cottage. Had that someone been a stranger, or a neighbor?

I shuddered, envisioning the cheerful red blossoms reflected in a spreading pool of blood, and turned to squelch disconsolately down the muddy path that would take me home.

I was halfway down the hill when the horse appeared.

Chapter 2

It came out of nowhere, a black stallion some fifteen hands high, bearing down on me like a runaway train. In my panicked attempt to get out of its way, I failed to remember how firmly my wellies were planted in the mud and jumped right out of my boots, landing flat on my back in a sodden mass of last year's leaves well mixed with this year's muck.

While I lay there dazed and winded, gasping like a netted trout, the horse's rider brought the steed to a halt, dismounted, and flung himself to his knees beside me.

"Lori?" he cried. "Oh, Lori, are you hurt?"

A gloved hand touched my forehead and I found myself looking up into the violet eyes of a man whose life I'd saved just over a year ago.

When I'd first met Christopher Anscombe-Smith, he'd been unshaven, unshorn, half-starved, and dressed in rags.

He'd come a long way since then.

He was gainfully employed, for one thing,

as stable master at Anscombe Manor, the property next door to mine. He lived there, too, in a sparsely furnished flat opposite the stables. He'd shaved his beard and clipped his prematurely gray hair short, exchanged his rags for serviceable work clothes, and added flesh and muscle to his lean frame. His face — his extraordinarily beautiful face — which had once been gaunt and pale, was now glowing with good health. The most charitable part of me rejoiced to see him looking so well.

The rest of me was ready to strangle him.

"*Kit*," I wheezed. "You *maniac*. You could've *killed* me."

"I'd sooner kill myself," he murmured, unzipping his rain jacket. "Are you hurt?"

"I'm peachy." I pushed myself into a sitting position and caught my breath. "There's nothing I like better than wallowing in frozen mud."

Kit wrapped his jacket around me and helped me to my feet — my stockinged feet. I shivered violently as gooey fingers of frigid muck oozed through my socks.

"May I have my boots?" I asked through chattering teeth.

"I'll tie them to the saddle," said Kit. "I'm taking you home."

"On Zephyrus?" I eyed the stallion warily.

"Thanks, but I'd rather walk."

"You'll catch your death." Kit retrieved my wellies and brought the horse around. "Please don't argue, Lori. I feel badly enough as it is."

"But —"

Kit cut my protest short by sweeping me off of my feet and onto the horse's back, where I teetered precariously until he climbed up behind me and wrapped his arms around my waist.

"Lean back," he instructed. "I won't let you fall. Gently, now, Zephyrus . . ."

Zephyrus did go gently, and Kit kept me more or less upright, but the downhill journey was a trial nonetheless. I was a lousy horsewoman at the best of times and the steep grade took its toll as seldom-used muscles strained to keep my mud-covered bottom from slithering out of the saddle. By the time Kit tethered the stallion to the apple tree in my back garden, I was certain that I'd never walk again.

I was on the verge of demanding that Kit carry me into the cottage when I caught sight of Will and Rob gazing wide-eyed at us through the solarium's back door. Forcing a cheery smile, I slid gingerly from the saddle and hobbled toward the cottage on my own two frozen feet.

"I'll help you inside," Kit offered. "Then I'll be off."

"Oh, no, you won't." I seized his elbow. "You think I'd turn you loose on an unsuspecting public? You're a hazard to your own health and everyone else's." I tightened my hold. "You're coming inside to get dry and warm, and you're not leaving until you tell me what's wrong."

Kit looked away. "What makes you think something's wrong?"

I glared at him. "Do I look stupid? You were riding like a maniac up there. You *never* ride like a maniac. Ergo, something must be wrong." I tried to push my wet hair out of my eyes, smeared my forehead with mud, and heaved a long-suffering sigh. "Besides, your lips are turning blue. I can't let you go home with blue lips, so put Zeph in the shed and come inside."

After a moment's hesitation, Kit led the stallion around the side of the cottage to the shed, where he'd find everything he'd need to make Zephyrus comfortable.

I watched him go, then sloshed into the cottage, where my adoring sons greeted me with gales of merry laughter. A grimy, wet, and limping mummy was, evidently, the sort of sight gag two toddlers could really sink their baby teeth into.

Annelise took one look at me and ran to fetch an armload of towels.

It was growing dark by the time Kit and I sat down to eat. The boys were in bed, and Annelise had gone to spend the evening with her mother, so Kit and I had the kitchen to ourselves. Kit had exchanged his wet clothes for a flannel shirt and a pair of baggy sweatpants that had last graced my husband's much brawnier frame. I'd changed into jeans, a sweater, and my thickest pair of wool socks.

After tossing Kit's riding gear into the washer, I'd given Bill a quick call to fill him in on my overly eventful day. He'd been suitably shocked to hear about the murder, relieved to know that my encounter with Zephyrus had injured nothing but my dignity, and as puzzled as I was by Kit's carelessness. He wasn't one bit surprised by my determination to find out what was troubling Kit.

"You're his good angel," he'd reminded me. "God knows he needs one."

I wasn't feeling remotely angelic as I filled two bowls with homemade barley soup. I was stiff and sore and convinced that certain parts of my anatomy would be black-and-blue by morning.

"I left a message for the Harrises at their hotel in Devon." It was the first time Kit had spoken since we'd entered the kitchen. "To let them know where I was. In case they call home."

Emma and Derek Harris, Kit's employers, owned Anscombe Manor. They lived there with Derek's teenaged children, Peter and Nell.

"Good idea," I said. "I wouldn't want them to worry." I set the ladle aside and covered the stockpot. "Not that there's anything to worry about."

"Lori —"

"Eat your soup," I ordered. I placed the brimming bowls on the table and pushed a plate of sandwiches toward him. "I'm not allowed to badger a hungry man. It's a violation of the Geneva Convention."

It was a violation of my own conscience as well. No matter how fit Kit seemed, I could never completely forget the sick and starving stranger who'd collapsed in my driveway just over a year ago. Even now there was something fragile about him, an air of vulnerability that brought out the latent lioness in me. However annoyed I was with him at the moment, I'd never let him go hungry again, and I'd cheerfully dismember anyone foolish enough to hurt him.

Kit ate mechanically, dutifully, as if he were more concerned with pleasing me than appeasing his appetite. I let him finish his meal in peace, but when the empty dishes were in the sink, I returned to the subject that was foremost in my mind.

"Bill's in London," I said, gazing intently at Kit across the kitchen table, "and Annelise is at her mother's. It's just you and me, old friend, so spill the beans. Tell me why you were riding hell-bent for leather up on Pouter's Hill."

Kit sat with his forearms on the table, his graceful, long-fingered hands lying one atop the other. "I don't think you can help this time, Lori. I don't think anyone can."

"I can try," I offered.

He was silent for what seemed a long time. Suddenly, his eyes flashed and his hands tightened into fists.

"It's that Hooper woman," he muttered. "If I'd known what damage she'd cause, I'd have killed her myself."

Chapter 3

My heart caromed off my ribcage. "Y-you didn't, did you?" I stammered. "Kill her, I mean."

"No, more's the pity." Kit thumped the table with a fist. "But if they ever catch the man who did, I'll be the first in line to shake his hand."

I'd never seen Kit angry before. I'd never imagined he could *be* angry, but there was no mistaking the expression on his face. He was *livid*. For a fleeting moment I felt strangely in awe of Mrs. Hooper. It would take a preternaturally offensive woman to ignite such fury in someone as gentle as Kit.

"Kit," I said cautiously. "Did Mrs. Hooper do something to upset you?"

He gave a short, mirthless laugh, then looked me straight in the eye. "Because of Mrs. Hooper, Nell Harris has declared her love for me."

A snort of involuntary laughter escaped before I could suppress it. "Nell thinks she's in love with you? What's so bad about that?"

"Everything," Kit said grimly. "When a fifteen-year-old girl pursues a thirty-year-old man, it's generally assumed that he's done something to encourage her. Every time I go into the village I'm met with a barrage of sly winks or reproachful scowls. It's been hell."

His words sobered me. For a man who valued privacy as highly as Kit did, such scrutiny would be intolerable, but even I could see why his way of life invited speculation.

Kit was a loner who lived apart from the village and whose job required little supervision. He was an exceptionally good-looking single man, yet he had no fiancée or steady girlfriend. And everyone knew that he spent a lot of time alone with Nell, whose love of horses rivaled his own. My friend was, in short, a scandalmonger's dream.

"How do you know Mrs. Hooper's responsible?" I asked.

"Nell told me," Kit replied. "She said she hadn't intended to declare her love until her sixteenth birthday, God help me, but that Mrs. Hooper had urged her to speak sooner. I've since learned that Mrs. Hooper mentioned Nell's intentions to several of her chattiest neighbors — purely out of concern for Nell's well-being, you understand."

With a sickening jolt I suddenly understood what Annelise had meant by "wicked" rumors. A few well-placed, evil whispers would be enough to brand Kit as a predator in the minds of people who'd never even met him.

"Nell's had a crush on me ever since I started working for the Harrises," Kit went on, "but I was oblivious. I thought she liked working with horses."

"Nell loves horses," I reminded him.

"And me, apparently," Kit muttered.

I rested my chin on my hand and frowned in puzzlement. "Why would Nell listen to Mrs. Hooper?"

"Mrs. Hooper could be charming," Kit told me. "She could be very charming and very persuasive when it suited her purpose."

"She seems to have charmed the vicar and his wife," I acknowledged. "But the Buntings are a power couple in Finch. They have position and influence. Why would she go after Nell?"

"To get back at me." Kit ran his hand through his short hair. "I wouldn't let her grandson ride Zephyrus. She brought him to the stables one day, a spoilt brat as wide as he is tall, and demanded that he be allowed to canter about on my horse."

"Was she *nuts?*" I exclaimed. "Zeph would have tossed the kid on his head."

"That's what I told Mrs. Hooper, and she seemed to understand. She was all smiles and good wishes when she left — all charm. A week later — on Christmas Eve, in fact — Nell came to me with her ridiculous declaration. I can only assume that it was Mrs. Hooper's idea of revenge." Kit cast his eyes heavenward and groaned. "It's ludicrous, Lori. Even if I were interested in pursuing a relationship — which I am not — I wouldn't do so with a *child*."

"A child," I echoed thoughtfully. It wasn't a word I'd have chosen to describe Emma's stepdaughter.

Lady Eleanor Harris wasn't your average gawky teenager. She was tall, willowy, and as ethereally beautiful as frost upon a windowpane. Her eyes were the color of a midnight sky, and her golden curls seemed to catch sunlight even on the cloudiest of days. She was graceful, engaging, formidably intelligent, and secure enough to hold her own with any adult. Nell had a fey quality that might make her seem childlike to the untrained eye, but those of us who knew her best had long since learned — sometimes to our cost — that she was wise beyond her years.

"She's still in *school*, for pity's sake," Kit was saying. "I'd never —"

"I know you wouldn't," I soothed.

Kit's face grew pensive. "She sends love poems to me. Passionate ones. In scented envelopes. Peggy Taxman looks daggers at me every time I set foot in the Emporium."

"Poor Kit," I said, trying hard not to smile.

"It's not funny," Kit scolded, reading my expression.

"I know it's not, honestly I do." I patted his hand. "But I'm afraid you're going to have to grin and bear it. Nell will grow out of it, I promise you."

"And in the meantime?" Kit's delicately curved mouth was set in a thin line. "I thought the situation had finally sorted itself out, but only this week I've gotten three abusive phone calls. Some wag rang this morning to ask if he could help me break in fillies."

"So that's what set you off," I said. "That's why you were up on Pouter's Hill."

"I was . . . angry. I don't like being angry." Kit lowered his long lashes and took a tremulous breath. "Lori," he said, "I've been offered a job at a racing stable in Norfolk. I'm seriously considering —"

"No," I interrupted. "Absolutely not."

"But Lori —"

"You're not going anywhere, Kit," I said

28

sternly. "You love Anscombe Manor, you love your job, and you have friends here who love you. You're not going to give all of that up because of a spiteful woman and a moonstruck schoolgirl."

Kit lifted his hands helplessly. "I don't know what else to do."

"You can stand up for yourself," I snapped. "Do you think you're the first person to trip over the village grapevine? Gossip's as common as clover in Finch."

"But a man in my position —"

"Do Emma and Derek believe that you've been flirting with their daughter?" I asked.

"Would I still be employed by them if they did?" Kit returned.

"That settles it," I declared. "I trust you, Bill trusts you, and Nell's parents trust you. The only people who don't trust you are the ones who don't know you, and they can each and every one of them take a flying leap into the river." I smacked the table with my palm. "Including and most especially *Peggy Taxman!*"

Kit's violet eyes flickered, and a sweet smile slowly crept across his face. "She'd make quite a splash."

I hesitated, caught off guard by his smile, then grinned back at him ruefully. "She'd drain the river."

"That would be a sight worth seeing," he observed.

"You bet it would." I took a breath. "So don't even think about going to Norfolk, okay?"

"I wouldn't dare." Kit glanced up as a flurry of wind-driven rain lashed the window above the sink.

"It's supposed to blow itself out by morning," I said, following his gaze. "Stay here for the night."

"I can't." Kit sighed wearily. "With Emma and Derek in Devon, there'll be no one to look after the horses in the morning."

"I'll call Annelise's brother. Lucca's helped out before. He knows the ropes." I put my hand over Kit's. "Stay. I'll make up a bed for you on the sofa."

"Alright. I will. I wasn't looking forward to the ride home. My anger kept me warm before, but for some reason I don't feel quite so furious anymore." He twined his long fingers with mine. "I've missed you, Lori. I've missed your magnificent roar."

"I've missed you, too," I gave his hand a reassuring squeeze. "Leave the anger to me, Kit. I'm much better at it than you are."

"I'll look in on Zephyrus, then have an early night." Kit sank back in his chair and raised his hand to massage the nape of his neck. "I haven't slept properly since Christmas."

I noted the dark shadows beneath his wide-set eyes and felt the lioness surge within me. Kit was kind and good and utterly defenseless. He'd done nothing but protect Mrs. Hooper's grandson from harm, and she'd repaid him with a sneaky-mean attack on his reputation.

If she'd walked into my kitchen at that moment, I'd've been sorely tempted to reach for the nearest blunt instrument.

Chapter
4

The storm raged throughout the night, but its fury was spent by daybreak. The sun rose on a glistening world of puddles and rain-stippled hedgerows. The air was sweet, the sky a shimmering blue, with only a smattering of ragged clouds to remind us of the gale that had blown the day before. April in the Cotswolds was nothing if not changeable.

Kit was fast asleep when Annelise and I brought the twins downstairs for breakfast. Will and Rob adored the stable master and threatened to lay siege to the sofa, but I distracted them with cinnamon toast and a trip to the shed to feed Zephyrus, then kept them occupied in the kitchen baking bread. I didn't want them to disturb Kit's first sound sleep since Christmas.

He was still dead to the world when the doorbell rang at half past eleven, heralding the arrival of Lilian Bunting and her nephew. I trotted up the hallway, hoping that little Nicky would be moderately well behaved. I didn't want him disturbing Kit's rest, either. I paused to peep in at Kit's slumbering form, then opened the front door.

A man stood on the flagstone path, clad in a black trench coat. He was in his mid-thirties, about six inches taller than me and slightly built. His hair, an innocuous shade of brown enlivened by vagrant strands of gold, fell in tight waves from a severe center part nearly to his shoulders, as if he were ashamed to show his ears or had never quite outgrown his hippie youth. He had a craggy, unhandsome face, with a pronounced jawline and a nose that looked as if it had been broken more than once, but his eyes were wonderful, a glimmering shade of sea-green flecked with blue and gold. They smiled before his mouth did.

"Hello," he said. "I'm Nicholas Fox. I believe you're expecting me."

"Nicky?" I blinked in confusion.

"Nicholas, please," he said. "I left Nicky behind when I left prep school."

"But . . . you're not a child," I faltered.

"I was once," he said brightly. "And I've been accused of behaving childishly on occasion. Shall I demonstrate?"

I laughed and invited him in.

"Sorry about the misunderstanding," I said, closing the door behind him. "From

33

the way Lilian talked about you, I thought you were a little boy."

"Dear Aunt Lilian," he said. "I'll always be Nicky to her. You, I presume, are Lori Willis."

"Lori Shepherd," I corrected. "Willis is my husband's last name, not mine, but we can simplify the whole thing by sticking with Lori."

"Lori it is, then. My aunt misinformed me as to your last name. Distress is scattering her wits, I fear. She did, however, tell me that you have two little boys of your own." His gaze flickered downward. "I can see for myself that it's true. Bakers, are they?"

I looked down and saw that my blue jeans were liberally sprinkled with small, floury handprints. I laughed again and offered to take Nicholas's trench coat. He'd dressed casually and for warmth, layering a heathery brown tweed blazer and deep blue V-neck sweater over a pale blue button-down shirt. I glanced with trepidation at his dark brown trousers and reminded myself to wash the boys' hands before they made his acquaintance.

"We've been baking bread," I informed him, "but I was about to start working on lunch. I hope you've brought an appetite with you."

"I'm sure I have one here somewhere," said Nicholas, patting his pockets.

I was in the middle of my third laugh when Kit emerged from the living room, tousled and barefoot and wearing a pair of Bill's striped pajamas.

When Nicholas extended his hand to shake Kit's, I noticed that his knuckles were scarred and misshapen, as if he'd beaten his fists against a brick wall.

"Nicholas Fox," he said. "Lilian Bunting's nephew. You must be Bill."

"No, he's not," I said, tearing my gaze from those battered hands. "My husband's in London. This is my friend Kit."

"Ah." Nicholas gently cleared his throat.

Kit broke the pregnant silence by clasping Nicholas's awkwardly hovering hand. "I'm Kit Smith," he said. "I run the stable yard at Anscombe Manor. Lori was kind enough to put my horse and me up for the night when we were caught out in the storm."

"Pleased to meet you," said Nicholas.

I directed Kit to the master bedroom, where I'd laid out his dry clothes, advised him that lunch would be ready in ten minutes, and brought Lilian's nephew with me to the kitchen.

Nicholas Fox was impressively well prepared to spend an afternoon with toddlers.

His pockets were stuffed with tiny cars, plastic farm animals, and a host of windup toys guaranteed to win my sons' affection. He, in turn, seemed delighted by Will and Rob.

I watched him from the corner of my eye as I threw together a salad-soup-and-sandwich meal. He clearly enjoyed roughhousing with the twins, and ate his lunch with equal relish, complimenting me on the fresh-baked bread as well as the blackberry crumble I'd whipped up for dessert. I couldn't understand why Lilian found her nephew so difficult to entertain. He didn't seem to be all that hard to please.

Kit left for Anscombe Manor as soon as the table was cleared, and Annelise took the twins outside to play. Nicholas offered to accompany them, but I shook my head and invited him to sit with me in the living room instead.

"Pace yourself," I advised, "or you'll be dropping in your tracks by the time you leave."

He bowed his head. "I defer to the expert, but they are charming children. And you have a lovely home."

"Thanks." Nicholas had so far praised my sons, my cooking, and my cottage. If he was trying to endear himself to me, he was succeeding. I gestured for him to take a seat in Bill's armchair and knelt to light the fire. "Do you have a family of your own?"

"Apart from the one I was born into, no," he replied. "No wife, no fiancée, and no prospects in the offing. I'm singularly single. I don't even own a cat."

"I didn't mean to pry," I said, blushing. "I only asked because you're so good with Rob and Will." I eyed his tweed blazer. "Are you a teacher?"

"Of a sort," he said. "I teach self-defense."

My gaze shifted to his scarred knuckles. "Karate? Judo? That sort of thing?"

"I'm small but deadly," he said, his eyes twinkling. "I've no students at the moment, so I thought I'd pay a visit to Aunt Lilian. I haven't been to Finch in years. As I live in London, I was rather hoping for a bit of peace and quiet."

"Instead of which you walked straight into the crime of the century." I was joking, but Nicholas didn't laugh.

"It's truer than you think," he commented. "According to Aunt Lilian, there hasn't been a murder in the village of Finch since one shepherd whacked another with the hook of his crook in the autumn of 1879. Since then there's been a number of deaths by misadventure but not a single murder."

I sat back on my heels. "So Mrs. Hooper's murder really *is* the crime of the century?"

"It is. Finch has had an exceptionally tranquil history." He paused. "Until now."

I got to my feet and made myself comfortable in the overstuffed armchair facing Nicholas's across the hearth. "No wonder the vicar's so upset. He must feel terrible, knowing that Finch's first major crime in over a hundred years happened on his watch."

"The murder shocked Uncle Teddy, naturally," said Nicholas, "but I believe he's even more troubled by the villagers' reactions to it."

"How have they reacted?" I asked, though I already had an inkling.

"With distinct indifference," he answered. "They seem to be taking Mrs. Hooper's death very much in stride."

"Good riddance to bad rubbish," I murmured, half to myself.

"Pardon?"

I raised my voice. "It's something my nanny said. About Mrs. Hooper . . ."

I turned toward the fire and began to tell Nicholas what I'd learned about the unpopular Mrs. Hooper. I repeated Mr. Barlow's observations on women who cause trouble wherever they go; recounted Annelise's hints about mischief and wicked rumors; and shared, with increasing indignation, the unfortunate results of Kit's attempt to protect Mrs. Hooper's grandson from Zephyrus. Nicholas listened without interruption, almost without blinking, his craggy face a sober mask of concentration.

"Mr. Barlow hit the nail on the head," I concluded. "Pruneface Hooper was as sneaky-mean as they come. She simpered to Kit's face while she stabbed him in the back. I wish I'd been home when the rumors started. If I'd known what she was up to, I'd've wrung her neck."

"Would you?" Nicholas said mildly.

I looked up, startled. I'd forgotten that he was in the room. "How did you do that?"

"Sorry?" he said.

"You disappeared into the woodwork while I was talking," I said. "How'd you do it? Is it some kind of Far Eastern mind-body-control thing?"

"I teach Zen and the art of listening," he said gravely. "I can also charm snakes and levitate."

"Yeah, right." I wrinkled my nose at him. "Too bad you weren't on hand to charm Pruneface. And to answer your question, no, I probably wouldn't have strangled her, but I definitely would have given her a piece of my mind."

"Of that I have no doubt." Nicholas rested his elbows on the arms of his chair and tented his fingers. "I wonder if Mrs. Hooper spread the same kind of rumor about someone else in Finch — someone less amiable than Mr. Anscombe-Smith."

"You mean someone who might have reacted violently?" I sighed. "It's possible, I suppose. I don't like the idea, but it's hard to avoid."

"Indeed." Nicholas tapped the tips of his index fingers together.

"You'd think the police would've figured it out by now," I said. "It's been ten days — eleven now — and the killer's still on the loose."

Nicholas got to his feet and strolled over to peer out of the bow window. He complimented me on the pleasant view, then added conversationally, "Did you know that Aunt Lilian's goddaughter is a file clerk at the local constabulary?"

"Is she?" My eyebrows rose. "How useful."

"If young Imogen is to be believed, the police are having a difficult time." Nicholas turned toward me. "They've found no forensic evidence in Crabtree Cottage, and the villagers have been strikingly unforthcoming during interviews. Furthermore, no one has come forward with information."

40

"There are no witnesses?" I said, astonished.

"None." Nicholas moved slowly around the room, pausing before a framed watercolor Bill had given me for Christmas. He inclined his head toward the painting. "Lesley Holmes?"

"Yes," I said. "She painted a series of watercolors in Finch last summer. I'm fond of her work."

"As am I." Nicholas took a backward step to admire the watercolor at arm's length. "It's Crabtree Cottage, isn't it?"

"It was done before Mrs. Hooper moved in," I said hastily.

"I thought as much." He gazed at the painting a moment longer, then returned to his chair. "No geraniums."

"Nicholas," I said impatiently, "what you said before, about there being no witnesses — it's absurd. Someone must have seen something. Nothing goes unnoticed in the village."

"Murders do, apparently." Nicholas rested his head against the back of the chair. "That's why Uncle Teddy's worked himself into a lather. The most heinous of crimes has been committed, a crime against God as well as man, and no one seems to care."

Theodore Bunting was a peace-loving

soul, but he also possessed a temper. I'd felt his righteous fury only once, when his flock had ignored a homeless man in need of help — Kit, in fact. The vicar's sermon, on that occasion, had scorched the villagers' ears. I could easily imagine his reaction to their casual dismissal of a violent death.

"Is your uncle fuming?" I asked.

"He alternates between fuming and brooding," Nicholas replied. "Aunt Lilian's afraid he'll make himself ill if this affair isn't resolved soon."

A commotion arose in the hallway as my sons returned from their outdoor expedition. Since they'd explored every puddle in the back garden, I excused myself to give Annelise a hand with changing them into dry jammies and putting them down for their naps. When I returned to the living room, I found Nicholas talking on his cell phone. I retreated to the hallway to give him privacy, but he called for me to come in and ended his conversation rapidly.

"Aunt Lilian," he explained. "She and Uncle Teddy are back from the inquest. My cue to depart."

"It's been a pleasure meeting you," I said, walking him to the front door. "And the boys are googly-eyed. They're convinced that you're related to Santa Claus."

Nicholas pulled a pair of yellow dinosaurs from his breast pocket and handed them to me. "For Will and Rob when they awaken," he explained. "I have a reputation to maintain." He took his trench coat from the hall stand and folded it over his arm as he opened the door. "Thank you for a lovely afternoon, Lori. I hope we'll meet again before I leave."

"I'm sure we will," I said, and waved him on his way.

I watched as he backed his car out of the drive, then stood for a moment, savoring the lush scent of spring and contemplating our conversation.

I wondered if Nicholas Fox understood the extreme implausibility of the information he'd acquired. Could a man who lived in London understand life in a rural village, where there was no such thing as privacy, where no one was anonymous, and where gossip spread as quickly as spilt milk?

I closed the door and went into the living room, to stand before the painting of Crabtree Cottage. The news of my sons' first steps had reached Finch long before I'd made the announcement, and Bill's confidential client list was discussed routinely in Peacock's pub — yet no one knew a thing about the murder.

My gaze roved restlessly over the painting, from the cottage's green door to the delicate fringe of gingerbread adorning the stoop's half-roof, and finally came to rest on the drip molding above the multipaned front window. Mrs. Hooper had been struck down near that window, in full view of the square, in a village top-heavy with busybodies — yet no one had seen or heard a thing.

It didn't make a lick of sense to me.

It might, however, make sense to someone else. What I needed was a local expert on village matters, and as luck would have it, I knew exactly where to find one. I called to Annelise to keep an eye on the boys and made a beeline for the study.

It was time to consult Aunt Dimity.

Chapter
5

When I inherited the cottage Bill and I now called home, I also inherited a few surprises. The greatest of these was the ongoing presence of the cottage's former owner, a remarkable woman named Dimity Westwood.

Dimity Westwood had been my late mother's closest friend. They'd met in London while serving their respective countries during the Second World War, and maintained their friendship long after the bombs had stopped exploding. The letters they wrote to each other, recounting joys, sorrows, and the vital trivia of everyday life, were among my most treasured possessions.

I'd grown up hearing about Aunt Dimity, but only as a fictional character in a series of bedtime stories. I didn't learn about the real Dimity Westwood until after her death, when she bequeathed to me a considerable fortune, a honey-colored cottage in the Cotswolds, and a blue-leather–bound journal with blank pages.

It was through the blue journal that I first exchanged words with Aunt Dimity. As she had once written to my mother, so she now wrote to me, but from an address much closer to heaven than to Finch.

When I opened the blue journal, its pages came alive with Dimity's elegant script, an old-fashioned copperplate taught in the village school at a time when blacksmiths were abundant. I couldn't explain the unearthly phenomenon. I could only acknowledge, humbly and gratefully, that Dimity Westwood continued to be as remarkable in death as she had been in life.

A scant handful of people shared the secret of the blue journal. Bill, Kit, and Emma were among them, but Annelise was not, so I closed the study door before taking the journal from its niche on the bookshelves and settling with it in one of the pair of tall leather armchairs that flanked the hearth.

"Dimity?" I said, opening the book. "Are you there?"

Where else would I be? I've been waiting to welcome you home.

Guilt pricked my conscience as I watched the familiar lines of royal blue ink loop and curl across the page.

"I'm sorry," I said. "I should have come to you sooner."

There's no need to apologize, Lori.

"Oh, but there is," I told her. "Something's happened. Something incredible."

Do tell.

"There's been a murder, in Finch."

There was a lengthy pause. Then three words appeared, printed in letters so large, they filled nearly half the page.

MURDER? IN FINCH?!?

Dimity was among the most understanding of souls, but even she was a bit put out with me for taking a whole day and a half to inform her of the crime of Finch's century. By the time I finished bringing her up to speed, she'd stopped blotting the page, but I could tell by the way she crossed her T's that she was still a little peeved.

I don't believe for one moment that no one noticed anything out of the ordinary on the morning in question. Someone must have seen something.

"My words exactly," I said. "But no one's volunteered any information to the police." I leaned closer to the page and added, "If you ask me, the villagers are engaged in a conspiracy of silence."

There have been many conspiracies in Finch, my dear, but none of them have been silent. Quite the contrary.

47

"Then why hasn't anyone spoken out?" I asked.

They may not be speaking to the authorities, but I've no doubt that they're jabbering like magpies to each other.

"What do you think they're saying?" I coaxed.

My guess — and it is an educated one — is that the good people of Finch don't want the murderer to be caught. They believe that a contemptible woman got what she deserved, they know who the culprit is, and they've agreed to close ranks in order to protect one of their own.

I put a hand to my forehead, dizzied by Dimity's plain speaking. She'd done nothing more than summarize my own suspicions, but those suspicions still made me uncomfortable. I couldn't quite bring myself to believe that my law-abiding neighbors would take it upon themselves to act as judge and jury in a case involving a capital offense.

Well, my dear, what are you going to do about it?

The question took me by surprise. "What do you expect me to do about it? It's up to the police to catch criminals."

How? If Mr. Fox is correct, they have nothing to go on. I'm afraid the police won't identify the malefactor without our help.

"If you want to know who killed Mrs.

Hooper," I said reasonably, "why don't you . . . ask her? She's dead, isn't she? You have that much in common."

With all due modesty, my dear, I very much doubt that Mrs. Hooper and I are in the same place. A woman who would treat Kit so cruelly would almost certainly spend eternity in a location with which I, thankfully, have no contact whatsoever. I'm sorry, Lori, but we must rely on terrestrial means to identify the person or persons unknown. In my experience, murder is the culmination of a series of events, seen and unseen. You must marshal your resources and investigate those events.

"I have resources?" I said doubtfully.

You have Emma Harris. I'd like you to enlist her help. She has a fine analytical mind and she doesn't flap easily.

I agreed with Dimity's assessment of my friend. Emma Harris was an imperturbable font of common sense, which explained why we got along so famously. Her cool head provided a perfect foil for my sometimes overheated one.

"I think she and Derek are still in Devon," I said. "But I'll talk to her as soon as she gets back. May I ask what I'm enlisting her for?"

I want the two of you to visit the vicarage as soon as possible, in order to find out what happened at the inquest. Then I want you to make

49

the rounds in Finch. *You're both considered locals, and you, Lori, have been away. I'm sure people will be eager to bring you up-to-date on village matters. I want you and Emma to make it your mission in life to collect gossip.*

I read between the lines. "You want me and Emma to find out if Mrs. Hooper spread rumors about someone other than Kit."

Correct. I think that Mrs. Hooper was exactly what Mr. Barlow said she was: a troublemaker. If she managed to stir Kit, Annelise, and Mrs. Sciaparelli to anger, it's more than likely that she stirred others.

"And her stirring might have provoked her killer," I put in.

I believe so. Find the motive and you'll find the murderer — and the murderer must be found. Crime has a way of contaminating all who come in contact with it. We mustn't allow the infection to spread. Run along, now.

I waited until Dimity's handwriting had faded from the page, then stared meditatively into the middle distance. I would never have admitted it to Aunt Dimity, but I wasn't as sure as she was that the killer should be caught. Sometimes it was wiser to let sleeping dogs lie.

I closed the journal and considered my assignment. I doubted that Emma and I would discover any useful information, but what if we did? What if we unearthed a tidbit that led to the killer's arrest and conviction? Would the villagers forgive us for turning one of their own in to the police? Would I forgive myself?

I knew that I should sympathize with the victim, but the victim in this case had made the mistake of attacking one of my dearest and most defenseless friends. Granted, she'd done so with words alone, but words could cause wounds that lingered longer than those inflicted by sticks and stones. If I felt any sympathy at all, it was for the victim's victims.

With a troubled sigh, I returned the blue journal to the shelf.

"Well, Reginald," I said, addressing the pink-flannel rabbit who shared the blue journal's niche, "I've got my marching orders."

Some people might consider talking to a stuffed bunny a minor form of madness. To me, it was as natural as conversing with a book. Reginald had entered my life shortly after I'd entered the world, and I'd been speaking with him ever since. He was, like Nicholas Fox, a gifted listener.

"I just wish I knew for certain that I was marching in the right direction," I added worriedly.

Reginald's black button eyes remained impassive. He was much too wise a bunny to contradict Aunt Dimity.

"Okay," I said, "I'll recruit Emma, finagle an invitation to the vicarage, and —"

The telephone on the old oak desk interrupted my monologue. I answered it and felt a stab of anxiety as Kit's frantic voice broke into my greeting.

"Lori," he said urgently. "The police came to Anscombe Manor to question me. They seem to think that *I* killed Pruneface Hooper!"

Chapter
6

The police weren't entirely stupid. They'd gotten wind of the scandalous rumor Pruneface Hooper had invented about Kit, but their informant had given it a darker twist. The new version held that Mrs. Hooper had caught Kit in the act of abusing Nell Harris the day before the murder, when Nell had been home for a brief holiday from school. If the story were true, it would give Kit a clear motive for wanting to silence Mrs. Hooper. True or not, it had given the authorities the excuse they needed to question him.

To make matters worse, Kit had no one to vouch for his whereabouts on the morning of the murder, and the stables were chockablock with blunt instruments.

Emma and Derek Harris had returned from Devon to find their friend and employee under siege. They'd spoken up for him and summoned their solicitor to keep the police at bay, but the encounter had shaken Kit to the core.

I did what I could to calm him, then asked to speak with Emma.

"Can you believe everything that's happened since you left for Devon?" I asked, when she picked up.

"I wish we hadn't gone," she replied. "We should never have left Kit alone. First the rumors, then the phone calls, and now this. Derek and I are concerned about him, Lori. We're afraid he might do something drastic."

"Mrs. Hooper's dead," I reminded her. "It doesn't get a whole lot more drastic than that."

"Not to Mrs. Hooper," Emma said, exasperated. "To *himself*. I don't think he can take much more."

"For God's sake," I said, clutching the phone, "you don't mean that he might hurt himself, do you?"

"That's exactly what I mean," Emma said grimly. "He'd hoped to escape this mess by leaving Anscombe Manor, but the police have requested — politely but pointedly — that he stay put. Kit feels trapped and persecuted and . . . I don't know what he might do."

"You keep an eye on him," I told her.

"I intend to," she declared. "Derek and I won't leave home until the police catch the real culprit."

I wasn't even vaguely tempted to mention Aunt Dimity's plan. If Emma couldn't join me in my quest to find the killer, I'd carry on alone. When I finished my conversation with her, I called Bill.

"The cops are picking on Kit because he's an easy target," I insisted, after filling him in on the latest turn of events. "They don't have a scrap of evidence."

"How do you know?" asked Bill.

"Lilian Bunting's goddaughter —"

"The village grapevine," Bill interrupted. "I should have guessed." He sighed. "Tell Kit to sit tight. Derek's solicitor is more than capable of dealing with a case of police harassment."

"What about the other harassment?" I demanded. "Some creep has accused Kit of being a child molester."

"It's gotten out of hand," Bill agreed, "but there's not much we can do about it except stand by Kit." There was a pause. "Lori, I'm sorry, but I have to go. Gerald's come in with a client."

"Okay," I said, making a heroic effort not to grumble. "I'll see you on Saturday."

"Lori," Bill said. "As long as Kit has you and Emma and Derek to defend him, he doesn't need a solicitor. I'll be home soon, love."

I hung up the phone, sat back, and lifted my gaze to the blue journal. Reginald sat beside it, his black button eyes gleaming imperiously, as if to remind me of the folly of second-guessing Aunt Dimity.

Because Dimity had been right. The crime's infection was spreading in Finch, poisoning hearts and minds. Things would go from bad to worse as long as the killer remained at large. Kit was already cracking under the strain. If the crime wasn't solved soon, he might break down completely.

I snatched up the phone and savagely punched the Buntings' number. I no longer cared who I sent to prison. I had to find out who'd killed Pruneface Hooper before Pruneface Hooper's murder killed my friend.

I left Annelise in sole charge of the boys the following morning and drove my canary-yellow Range Rover toward the village. Lilian Bunting had invited me to lunch at the vicarage, but I'd left two hours earlier than necessary. I wanted to make a stop along the way and knew from past experience that it might take a while.

Ruth and Louise Pym were identical twin sisters who lived about a mile outside of Finch. They were well into their nineties, yet they somehow managed to stay as spry as sparrows. They drove their own car, won flower-show blue ribbons for their chrysanthemums, and knew which way the wind blew in the village. Their minds sometimes meandered along unfathomable paths, but there was always a point to the journey, and it was always one worth waiting for.

Their house, unlike most in the area, was made of mellow orange-red brick, with lattice windows and a neatly trimmed thatch roof that had weathered through the years to a mottled gray. Not one wall in the house was straight, not one floor was even, but the furniture had been there for so long that it had accommodated itself to the building's peculiarities — neither chairs nor tables wobbled, and no pictures hung askew.

I parked my car on the grassy verge and let myself through the wrought-iron gate between the Pyms' short hedges. The carefully tended flower beds bordering the path to the front door were alight with bright spring bulbs. Drifts of hyacinths, daffodils, and tender white narcissi turned their faces to the sun like a choir praising the miracle of spring. I paused on the doorstep to survey the lovely scene before turning the key-shaped handle on the old-fashioned bell.

The door opened. One sister appeared,

then the other, but it was beyond my poor powers of observation to figure out who was who. Both were dressed in long-sleeved gowns of the palest dove-gray wool, with four flat pleats falling from crocheted collars to tiny, cinched-in waists. Their shoes were black and extremely sensible, and their white hair was caught up in identical buns on the backs of their identical heads. I'd long since learned to rely on my ears rather than my eyes to tell the sisters apart: Louise's voice was softer, and Ruth invariably spoke first.

"Two visitors in one morning!" Ruth exclaimed. "And such . . ."

". . . welcome ones," Louise continued. "Come in, come in, dear Lori, and tell us about . . ."

". . . your voyage to America!" Ruth finished. The sisters' Ping-Pong speaking style required the listener to have an agile neck.

I returned their greetings and handed each a tissue-wrapped length of Brussels lace. "My father-in-law sends his best wishes," I said, "and hopes that you'll forgive the tardy arrival of his Christmas presents."

Ruth beamed up at me. "We'll consider them . . ."

". . . early Easter gifts," Louise promised, "and cherish the giver. Now, do come in, Lori, and let us . . ."

". . . introduce you to our other guest." Ruth drew me into the sitting room, but there was no need to make an introduction. I'd already met their other guest.

Nicholas Fox's eyes smiled as he rose from his chair at the tea table. He was wearing blue jeans, a creamy turtleneck, and his trusty brown tweed blazer.

"We meet again," he said.

"I thought we would," I replied, disconcerted, "at lunch."

"Ah, but it was such a beautiful morning," he said, "I couldn't resist a stroll."

Ruth stood between us, her bright bird's eyes darting from my face to Nicholas's. "Dear Nicholas walked all the way . . ."

". . . from the vicarage," said Louise. "We were in the front garden when he passed . . ."

". . . and he said such splendid things about our hyacinths," Ruth went on, "that we simply had to ask him in for a cup of tea. Do be seated, both of you."

Nicholas moved a sturdy Queen Anne chair to the tea table for me before resuming his own seat, and the sisters took their places facing us.

The modestly proportioned walnut table was trembling under the weight of the Pym sisters' "cup of tea." Three plates of crustless sandwiches vied with a pair of overladen pastry stands and an exquisite tea set painted — by the sisters' own hands, I suspected — with a sprinkling of dew-dappled strawberries.

While Louise busied herself with the teapot, Ruth pressed me to sample the goodies. I conscientiously filled a dish and hoped that Lilian Bunting was preparing a light lunch.

"We didn't recognize Nicholas at first," Ruth informed me. "He was much younger . . ."

". . . the last time he came to visit his dear aunt," said Louise, "and his delightful hair was much, much shorter."

"I don't see my aunt and uncle as often as I should," Nicholas acknowledged. "London's an all-absorbing sort of place. It's far too easy to forget that the rest of the world exists."

"We've never been to London," said Ruth. "But we've heard that it's . . ."

". . . rather large and terribly exciting," Louise commented. "Our small community must seem . . ."

". . . distressingly dull by comparison," Ruth concluded.

"Not at all," said Nicholas. "Finch is a charming village."

"And it's had its share of excitement

lately," I put in. "I can't tell you how surprised I was to hear about what happened to Mrs. Hooper."

A chill seemed to pass through the room as the Pyms' lips primmed into identical thin lines of disapproval. Nicholas, who'd been contentedly gorging himself on the sisters' feather-light éclairs, suddenly became as still as stone.

"That's because you didn't know her, dear," said Ruth. "She was a most . . ."

". . . objectionable woman." Louise sipped her tea before adding, "Her wake was an almost silent affair. Since no one wished to speak ill of the dead . . ."

". . . no one spoke," said Ruth. "Apart from the vicar, of course, and Mrs. Hooper's son. It reminded us of the hermit's wake . . ."

". . . though he hadn't a son to speak for him," Louise informed us, "and people were silent then not because they disliked the poor fellow but because so little was known about him."

"No one seems to know anything about Mrs. Hooper's death, either," I prompted hopefully, but Ruth went on as if I hadn't spoken.

"The hermit was antisocial in his way," she observed, "just as Mrs. Hooper . . ."

". . . was antisocial in hers," said Louise.

"The difference being that the hermit's ways harmed no one, whereas . . ."

". . . Mrs. Hooper's did a great deal of harm." Ruth offered me a slice of seedcake. "The truly regrettable thing is that she continues . . ."

". . . to do so much harm after her death." Louise refilled Nicholas's cup.

"Did she harm you?" Nicholas asked.

"She was a serpent in the bosom of our village," Louise declared. "My sister and I know how to deal with serpents."

The seedcake, of which I was very fond, seemed to turn to chalk in my mouth. I'd never heard the Pyms speak so bluntly about anyone.

"One avoids them," said Ruth.

"As we avoided Mrs. Hooper," added Louise. "Others did not and were stung . . ."

". . . rather severely." Ruth brushed a crumb from the tablecloth. "And now they sting each other. That's the trouble, you see. Questions . . ."

". . . so many unanswered questions." Louise tilted her head to one side. "And gingerbread, of course."

I glanced uncertainly at Nicholas, but his eyes were fixed on Louise's.

"Did you say . . . gingerbread?" I ventured.

"Gilded gingerbread." Louise nodded. "We make it every year . . ."

". . . to give as gifts at Eastertide." Ruth's nod mirrored her sister's. "Our motor isn't functioning properly, however, and since Mr. Barlow is away from home —"

"He is?" I interrupted. I'd been counting on a conversation with the prophetic mechanic.

"He's visiting family, we believe," said Ruth. "Somewhere up north. Naturally, we wouldn't trust our motor to anyone but Mr. Barlow, so we were rather hoping . . ."

". . . that you would do us a great favor," said Louise, "and deliver the gingerbread for us. There's no hurry. It will keep for several days. We've written the names of the recipients . . ."

". . . atop each box," Ruth concluded.

Nicholas deposited his empty plate on the table and stood. "Ladies," he announced, "I am at your service."

"Me, too," I piped up hastily. "We can use my car to make the deliveries. And if you need to go anywhere, please give me a call."

"So kind, so kind," the sisters chorused.

The Pyms were acquainted with everyone who lived in and around Finch and were known for their generosity, so I expected to fill the Range Rover to the roof with gingerbread. I was puzzled, therefore, when Nicholas returned from the kitchen carrying only six boxes.

"Shall we come back for the rest?" I asked hesitantly.

Ruth smiled. "We wouldn't dream of . . ."

". . . imposing on you further." Louise fell silent, her bright eyes gleaming like polished river stones.

Nicholas took the hint. "I'm afraid that Lori and I must run or we'll be late for Aunt Lilian's lunch — which you've spoilt, dear ladies, in a most delightful way. Your marvelous éclairs have rendered me incapable of doing justice to my aunt's cooking."

The Pyms' softly wrinkled cheeks grew pink with pleasure, and I gave Nicholas an admiring glance. He was as good with elderly spinsters as he was with nearly-two-year-old boys. After we said our good-byes to Ruth and Louise, I offered him a lift back to the vicarage.

"Or would you prefer to walk off those marvelous éclairs?" I added, opening the gate.

"I'd appreciate a lift, thank you," he answered. "I believe I've had enough fresh air for one morning. My London lungs aren't quite sure what to do with it."

A *ping* sounded on my internal radar, and

I watched Nicholas closely as he loaded the boxes of gingerbread into the Range Rover's rear compartment. I recalled his sudden stillness when the subject of the murder had arisen and the single, telling question he had asked. Had he happened on the Pyms by accident? Or had he insinuated himself into their home with a clear intent in mind?

"Nicholas," I said, closing the rear door, "was it really the fresh air that brought you here?"

"It might have been." He leaned back against the Rover. "You must admit that it's a plausible excuse."

I frowned. "An excuse for what?"

"I should've thought it was obvious." The gold flecks in his eyes glittered as he inclined his head toward me. "Since you and I came here for precisely the same reason."

Chapter
7

My internal radar started clanging, but I wasn't ready to show my hand just yet.

"What reason would that be?" I inquired politely.

Nicholas eyed me skeptically, then launched into a passable imitation of my American accent. "Why, Miss Pym, I can't tell you how shocked I was to hear about the murder. Isn't it strange, Miss Pym, that no one seems to know a thing about the murder?" He shook his head as if gravely disappointed. "If you were a barrister, you'd be admonished for leading the witnesses."

The mimicry was carried out so good-naturedly that I couldn't take offense.

"Okay," I admitted. "I came here to pick the Pyms' brains. I'm curious about Mrs. Hooper's death. Aren't you?"

"As I said, we both came here for the same reason." Nicholas checked his watch. "We're not due at the vicarage for a half hour, and I think my lungs could stand another liter or two of untainted oxygen. Let's stretch our legs."

A fitful breeze toyed with his long hair as we stepped away from the Rover. The hedgerows lining the narrow lane were heavy with morning dew, so we walked side by side down the middle of the road. There was no need to keep an eye out for traffic. The lane was so seldom used that we could have sunbathed on the faded center line.

While we walked, Nicholas talked. He told me that the inquest had done little more than confirm what his aunt and uncle — and everyone else in Finch — already knew: Mrs. Hooper had been struck on the head with a blunt instrument by a person or persons unknown between the hours of five and nine in the morning on Thursday, March 22.

She'd evidently been killed where she'd been found, in the front parlor of Crabtree Cottage. The cottage's doors and windows had been unlocked, but the police had found no evidence of theft. Finally, and perhaps most predictably, no locals had been on hand to offer testimony, apart from Peggy Taxman, who'd described finding the body.

"Mrs. Taxman had come to collect the rent, apparently," said Nicholas. "She and

Mrs. Hooper knew each other, back in Birmingham, before Mrs. Taxman came to live in Finch."

"She sounds like the kind of friend Peggy Taxman would have," I commented dryly.

"Mrs. Taxman is an imposing woman," Nicholas acknowledged.

"She's terrifying." I held up a cautioning finger. "If she so much as mentions the church fête, run the other way or you'll find yourself in charge of the pony rides."

"I see," said Nicholas, grinning, "an organizer. There's one in every village. Thanks for the warning."

"Don't mention it," I said, glad that, for once, I'd made him smile instead of the other way around.

The inquest's impact on the vicar was, alas, no laughing matter. The proceeding's inconclusive conclusions had left Theodore Bunting so depressed that he'd spent the previous evening brooding in his library, and so distracted that he'd skipped over the third collect in the morning service.

"I'm concerned about my uncle," Nicholas explained, "and somewhat underfoot at the vicarage, so I thought I'd lend the police a hand. Or at least a pair of ears. When Aunt Lilian mentioned the Pyms, it occurred to me that they might provide a starting point."

"They usually know what's what," I agreed. "And the police wouldn't have much luck questioning them."

Nicholas smiled wryly. "It takes a practiced ear to understand the Pyms."

We walked on in silence while I weighed the pros and cons of asking Nicholas to join forces with me. He'd already displayed a willingness to share information, and he knew how to listen. He was comfortable with all sorts of people, and as the vicar's nephew, he'd fit neatly into the constellation of relationships that formed the social fabric of the village. Moreover, I was comfortable with him. On the whole, I decided, he would make an admirable substitute for Emma.

"Nicholas," I said, coming to a halt, "I'm as worried about my friend Kit as you are about your uncle, and I've lost faith in the police. I didn't come here today out of idle curiosity. I want to find out who killed Pruneface Hooper." I bowed my head, let my shoulders slump, and emitted a melodramatic sigh. "The trouble is, my interrogation skills aren't what they used to be. I keep leading my witnesses." I peeked up at Nicholas and saw his eyes curve into half-moons as yet another smile wreathed his face. "I could use your help."

"As I could yours," he said. "Four ears are far better than two."

I wondered fleetingly what his ears looked like under those wavy curtains of hair, then turned to him and offered my hand. "Partners?"

"Partners," he repeated firmly.

"And may our next interview be more successful than our last," I added.

As we shook hands, I noticed the strength of his grip and the calloused ridge of skin that ran along the outside of his palm. If our inquiries roused any rabid dogs, I told myself, it would be comforting to have a self-defense expert in my corner.

With a scant ten minutes left before our lunch date at the vicarage, we made our way back to the Rover and took off for the village. We were nearly through the dangerous bend that curved around the Pyms' house when Nicholas spoke.

"I don't know that I agree with you about our first interview," he said. "I found it extremely informative."

"You did?" I said. "The Pyms didn't tell us anything new, unless you count the bit about the hermit's wake."

"Funny . . ." Nicholas pursed his lips meditatively. "I was under the impression that they'd provided us with a list of suspects."

I glanced at him so sharply that he had to catch hold of the steering wheel to keep me from swerving off the road.

"Did I miss something?" I asked, resuming control of the car. "When did they give us a list of suspects?"

"The gilded gingerbread." Nicholas looked over his shoulder toward the rear compartment. "There are only six boxes for the entire village. A somewhat inadequate supply, don't you agree? And not one is addressed to the vicarage. A curious omission, at Eastertide."

I nodded, but kept my eyes focused on the road. I'd already totaled one Range Rover in a fog-shrouded valley in Northumberland. Bill would never let me hear the end of it if I put so much as a dent in its replacement.

"Ruth and Louise gave us six boxes . . . and six names," I said. "Our suspects?"

"If not of the murder, then of withholding information." Nicholas faced forward. "The Pyms may not have held Mrs. Hooper in high esteem," he understated, "but they want her killer caught. They want answers to those unanswered questions, and they're doing what they can to point us in the right direction." He held up six scarred fingers. "Six directions, in fact: Billy Barlow, George Wetherhead, Miranda Morrow, Sally Pyne, Dick Peacock, and Peggy Taxman. Those

71

are the names on the boxes." He let his hands fall. "Do they suggest anything to you?"

"Yeah," I muttered. "They suggest that I'm going to have to get one friend in trouble in order to protect another. Ah, well," I went on, taking a deep breath, "I knew the job was dangerous when I took it."

"That's the spirit," Nicholas said bracingly. "Shall we begin our deliveries after lunch?"

"Tallyho," I said, and comforted myself with the knowledge of how pleased Aunt Dimity would be to hear that I'd finally marshaled a resource.

Finch's business district — such as it was — encircled an irregular oblong of lawn fringed by a ribbon of cobbles and adorned at one end by a Celtic cross, which served as a war memorial. As we bumped over the humpbacked bridge, I saw that the square was deserted. No one, it seemed, was in the mood to be out and about, enjoying the spring sunshine.

I cruised past the greengrocer's, the Emporium, and Peacock's pub, glanced over at Sally Pyne's tearoom and at Wysteria Lodge, which housed Bill's office, and slowed to a standstill when I came to Crabtree Cottage, next door to the pub, on the northwest corner of the square. Apart from a no-trespass notice posted on the front door, the cottage looked unchanged.

"The scene of the crime," Nicholas noted in suitably sonorous tones.

"It's not exactly buzzing with activity," I commented.

"I imagine the scene-of-crime team has picked it clean by now," said Nicholas.

Whatever the state of the investigation, someone was looking after the geraniums. The bloodred blossoms looked as stunning as they had in late December and swayed gently in their hanging pots, as if they'd just been watered. I craned my neck to see if I could spy a face beyond the multipaned window but saw no one.

A quick left turn took us into Saint George's Lane. I pointed out the old schoolhouse, which served as the village hall, and Mr. Wetherhead's home, which had once housed the schoolmaster. Each place held memories for me. I wondered how the memories would be altered if it turned out that one of those quaint buildings sheltered a killer.

The vicarage held the dearest memories of all. Bill and I had held our wedding reception in the rambling, two-story house, surrounded by friends, family, and hundreds of blue irises. I smiled reminiscently as I parked the Rover in the graveled parking space and followed Nicholas through the front door.

Lilian Bunting had evidently decided that luncheon would be a formal affair. The dining room, its wide windows overlooking the front garden and Saint George's Lane, was attired as resplendently as a bride. The table was draped with white linen, decked with old silver, and set with the Buntings' second-best china. A cut-glass vase bristling with bright yellow tulips served as a center-piece.

Lilian's grim visage detracted slightly from the tulips' radiance.

"Teddy refuses to join us for lunch," she announced as she entered the dining room. "He claims to have no appetite, though he scarcely ate a crust of bread at breakfast."

"Let me speak with him," Nicholas offered, and left us alone in the dining room.

"And let me speak with you," I said to Lilian, and told her of our plan to collect information on Mrs. Hooper's murder. "We may come up empty," I warned, "but anything's better than sitting back and doing nothing."

"You can't do worse than the authorities

have done," Lilian said. "And Nicky does have a way with people."

"I've noticed." I surveyed the sparkling table and decided to tell a minor lie in hopes of cheering Lilian further. "I'm really looking forward to this meal. I missed a lot of things while I was in the States, but your cooking was right at the top of the list."

"Don't be silly," said Lillian, but I could tell by the way she lifted her chin that I'd achieved my goal.

Lilian and I were filling the water glasses when Nicholas returned to the dining room, his uncle trailing dolorously in his wake.

The Reverend Theodore Bunting wasn't a little ray of sunshine at the best of times — his long face, dignified beak of a nose, and mournful gray eyes were better suited to funerals than to weddings — but I'd never seen him so utterly downcast. His shoulders sagged, his clerical collar was askew, and the faint lines in his forehead had deepened to ravines. He looked as though he'd aged ten years over the past three months.

"Nicholas tells me that you and he are trying to clear up this dreadful business," he said, shaking my hand. "My prayers will be with you. God knows the villagers won't speak honestly with their pastor."

"That's their loss," I said stoutly. "I don't

want you driving yourself into the ground because they're too stupid to know what's good for them."

"Listen to Lori." Nicholas took his uncle by the elbow and guided him to the head of the table. "It's your duty to stay fit. Your flock will need you more than ever when the truth of the matter comes out."

"If it does," the vicar murmured.

" 'Act as if ye have faith and faith shall be given unto you.' Oops." Nicholas gave the vicar a wily, unapologetic glance. "Sorry, Uncle Teddy, that's your line."

Theodore Bunting's mouth twitched with a suggestion of a smile, and Lilian beamed as happily as if her husband had burst into song. As I watched the vicar tuck into his green salad, I felt a surge of confidence in my newly launched joint venture.

Nicholas truly did have a way with people.

Chapter
8

The luncheon was more enjoyable than anyone could have anticipated. Lilian made sure that our conversation centered on my recent visit to the States — anything to divert her husband's attention from local events — while Nicholas and I attempted to polish off the roast beef, new potatoes, fresh asparagus, and assorted side dishes that Lilian had so lovingly prepared. We were attacking the dessert — a dreamy crème brûlée speckled with freshly ground vanilla beans — when I sat up abruptly and stared out of the window.

"You could charm the whiskers off a cat," I said to Nicholas. "How are you with dragons?"

"Undaunted," he owned.

"Then polish up your armor," I told him, "because we're about to do battle."

Nicholas followed my gaze in time to see Peggy Taxman walk determinedly past the vicarage. She was dressed in black from head to toe and gripped a cellophane-wrapped floral bouquet in both hands.

"She's going to the churchyard," said Lilian. "She goes there every day. She must be spending a small fortune on flowers."

"Worldly wealth is of little consequence when one has lost a friend," the vicar observed.

"Be that as it may," Lilian said tartly, "I've never known worldly wealth to be of little consequence to Mrs. Taxman."

While his aunt and uncle debated the point, Nicholas calmly finished his crème brûlée and put down his spoon.

"I've been meaning to pay my respects to the dead," he murmured. His sea-green eyes twinkled as he gave me a sidelong look. "Care to join me?"

"I'll bring the gilded gingerbread," I said. "You bring the graveside manner."

Saint George's Church stood at the top of Saint George's Lane in the midst of a manicured churchyard bounded by a low stone wall and entered by means of a shingle-roofed lych-gate. It was a tranquil place, crisscrossed with graveled paths, dotted with weathered tombs, and shaded in summer by two towering cedars of Lebanon.

Aunt Dimity's mortal remains were buried there, beneath a tangle of vines that would soon be awash in a froth of fragrant pink roses. I was irrationally pleased when I saw that her final resting place was nowhere near Mrs. Hooper's. I doubted there would ever be two less kindred spirits.

Saint George's newest grave had been dug at the front of the churchyard, in the tussocky southwest corner. We spotted Peggy Taxman standing over it as we came up the lane. She stood facing us but gazing downward, her eyes closed and hands folded, as if in prayer. By the time we'd passed through the lych-gate, she'd finished her devotions and stooped to tweak her most recent floral offering into a more pleasing position.

I crept toward her, bracing myself for the first blast of her voice. Peggy Taxman was neither tall nor unusually wide, and her attire was exactly what one would expect of a middle-aged woman in mourning, but the sheer force of her personality more than made up for her modest appearance. When she spoke, Finch trembled.

"Good afternoon, Peggy," I said, crossing to the far side of the grave. "Forgive me for intruding, but I wanted to let you know how sorry I was to hear about your friend."

"Thank you," she said in unnaturally subdued tones. She favored Nicholas with a measuring look as he came up beside me. "You're

Lilian Bunting's nephew. Nicholas, isn't it? You've been calling on the Pyms, I hear."

If Nicholas was surprised by Peggy's artless demonstration of the grapevine's efficiency, he didn't show it.

"The kind sisters took pity on a footsore rambler," he said politely.

"Did they take pity on you, too, Lori?" Peggy's eyes narrowed shrewdly behind her rhinestone-studded glasses. "I heard that you dropped in on them on your way to the vicarage."

"Ruth and Louise asked me to deliver their gilded gingerbread," I answered half-truthfully. I looked down at the grave to avoid Peggy's penetrating stare. The upright headstone, with its crisply carved inscription, stood in sharp contrast to its lichen-clad and crazily tilting neighbors. "Their motor, er, car isn't working."

"First I've heard of it," Peggy snapped. "I suppose they're waiting for Mr. Barlow to repair it. Did they say when he'd be back?"

"No," I replied. "The only thing they told us was that he'd gone up north to visit relatives."

"No one seems to know when he'll be back," Peggy grumbled. "It's suspicious, if you ask me."

"Why?" I asked.

"Don't you know?" Peggy barked. "Billy Barlow left town the same day Prunella died. At the crack of dawn, so I've heard. And no one's had a word from him since."

"No one would expect to hear from him," I reminded her. "Mr. Barlow never keeps in touch with anyone in Finch when he's away."

"That's as may be," Peggy growled irritably. "But what was he doing out there on the square so early in the morning? That's what I'd like to know. The police would, too, I've no doubt."

I quaked in my boots at the resurgence of Peggy's familiar, unsubdued personality but ventured gamely, "He was probably taking Buster for a walk before the drive up north."

Peggy scowled but admitted that I might be right. It was common knowledge that Mr. Barlow was mad about his terrier.

"Far be it from me to cast aspersions," Peggy intoned, "but no one can deny that Mr. Barlow didn't get on with Prunella."

"He must be hard to please," Nicholas observed. "My aunt and uncle told me that Mrs. Hooper was an admirable woman."

Peggy looked at him closely, as if suspecting sarcasm, but Nicholas's face betrayed nothing more than sincere sympathy.

"She *was* an admirable woman," Peggy

insisted. "She may not have been everyone's cup of tea, but she was a good friend to me."

"No one can be everyone's cup of tea," Nicholas reasoned.

"She took an interest in people," Peggy went on. "There's no harm in that, is there?"

"No harm at all," Nicholas soothed.

Peggy's gaze slewed toward me. "Seems she had good cause to take an interest in Nell Harris's welfare."

A red mist seemed to float before my eyes, and my grip tightened on the box of gingerbread. If Nicholas's elbow hadn't pressed lightly against mine, I would have made a heartfelt effort to knock Peggy Taxman's block off.

"I'm sure that Mrs. Hooper took an interest in everyone's welfare," he said. "I know that she was enormously helpful to my uncle. He thought the world of her floral arrangements."

"She wanted to be of service to the church," Peggy said earnestly, successfully diverted from making further snide remarks about Nell's so-called welfare. "If the vicar chose her to dress the font for Easter, it was because he knew she'd do it well. And if his decision put a certain person's nose out of joint, it wasn't Prunella's fault. Though to hear a certain person talk, you'd think

Prunella had plotted and connived to get the job."

"Which she would never do," Nicholas interjected, "because there was no need."

"No need at all." Peggy clasped her hands at her waist and sniffed haughtily. "Still, resentment can lead to anger, and anger to retaliation. I'm not saying that it did, mind you, but everyone knows that that it can. *Particularly*," she added, with a significant nod, "when a certain person is as short-tempered as a troll." She bent to give the cellophane-wrapped bouquet a final tweak, then straightened. "You must come by the Emporium, Nicholas. I'd like to introduce you to my husband."

"It would be an honor," said Nicholas. He pried my hands from the box of gingerbread and presented it to Peggy. "Please accept this gift from the Pyms with their best wishes for a joyous Easter — as joyous as it can be, under the circumstances."

"Thank you," Peggy said, accepting the tribute with regal dignity. "And welcome home, Lori. It'll be good to see you back in church on Sunday — you and *your husband*. He's back from London Saturday, isn't he? I'm sure you'll be glad to see him." Without deigning to wait for a reply, she marched out of the churchyard and down Saint George's

Lane, toward the square.

When she'd disappeared from view, Nicholas took me by the shoulders and subjected my face to a minute inspection. As his eyes darted from my forehead to my chin, I couldn't help thinking that his craggy features weren't so much homely as *interesting*, full of character, kindness, and a certain elemental strength.

"What are you doing?" I asked.

"Checking for scorch marks." He released his hold and stood back. "I think she may have singed your eyebrows with that last crack about your husband, but otherwise you seem to be unscathed. How about me?"

"I think Peggy wants to adopt you," I said, laughing. I sobered then and added quietly, "Thanks for steering her away from Kit. If you hadn't been here —"

"Anger would have led to retaliation," he finished sententiously, "as it so often does." He walked over to sit on the low stone wall. "What a remarkable performance. What was it the Pym sisters said? 'Mrs. Hooper stung her victims, and now they sting each other'? Mrs. Taxman is bubbling over with venom."

I kicked a clod of mud into a clump of grass. "It's amazing how many people she didn't cast aspersions on."

"Let's see," said Nicholas. "There's Mr. Barlow, who didn't get on with Mrs. Hooper and whose whereabouts are conspicuously unknown. There's Kit, the convenient scapegoat. And there's the certain person who resented Mrs. Hooper's church activities."

"The certain troll-tempered person?" I squashed another mud ball beneath my heel before walking over to sit beside Nicholas. "It's got to be Sally Pyne. She owns the tearoom, and she's always been in charge of decorating the baptismal font at Easter. I'll bet she was ready to spit tacks when the vicar gave the job to Pruneface."

"But was she ready to inflict bodily harm on the usurper?" Nicholas brushed his hair back from his face and let his gaze travel slowly around the churchyard.

The air was sweet and still and filled with birdsong. A pair of robins scouted the cowslips for worms, a chaffinch flickered from one tomb to another, and a flock of twittering cousins filled the cedars' wide-spread branches.

I settled myself more comfortably on the wall and mused aloud: "It doesn't seem right to mention violence in such a peaceful place."

Nicholas folded his arms. "I'm sure the dead don't mind."

"You'd be surprised," I quipped, and promptly wished the words unspoken.

It was too late, however. Nicholas was already giving me an inquisitive sidelong look.

"I'd be extremely surprised to learn that the dead mind anything," he said. "Wouldn't you?"

I fixed my gaze on Pruneface Hooper's grave and replied cautiously, "I've had some unusual experiences in England. It may sound crazy to you, but those experiences have led me to believe that a person's spirit can be quite active even after his body has turned to dust."

"Interesting." Nicholas pursed his lips, then shrugged nonchalantly. "Let's hope Mrs. Hooper's spirit isn't one that remains active. She caused more than enough trouble in the flesh."

I felt a surge of relief and gratitude, as if Nicholas had helped me leap a treacherous hurdle. Still, I was appalled by my indiscretion. I never breathed a word about my experiences with Aunt Dimity to any but the closest friends and family, yet here I was, discussing my views on the afterlife with a man I'd known for less than forty-eight hours.

"Nicholas," I said. "Has anyone ever told you that you're easy to talk to? Peggy doesn't usually confide in strangers, but she couldn't stop yammering at you. As for me, if I'm not careful, I'll wind up giving you my secret recipe for oatmeal cookies."

"I'd refuse to listen." Nicholas wrapped his arms around his stomach and groaned. "I'm far too full to even think about food."

"In that case, we'd better wait until tomorrow to do the tearoom," I said. "Because Sally Pyne will insist on feeding us, and everything she makes is rich and gooey."

Nicholas shuddered and readily agreed to meet me at the tearoom at ten the following morning. As we made our way back to the vicarage, I doubted that anyone's secrets would be safe for long from my secret weapon. Finch didn't stand a chance against the easygoing, charming Mr. Fox.

Chapter 9

I reported in to Aunt Dimity as soon as Annelise and I had put the twins to bed.

"We have liftoff," I announced upon opening the blue journal. "The investigation into the untimely death of Pruneface Hooper is under way."

Hoorah. Aunt Dimity's elegant copperplate curled and looped across the page without betraying undue signs of great excitement. *Have you garnered any useful tidbits?*

"Maybe." I leaned back in the leather armchair and put my feet up on the ottoman. "It seems that Mr. Barlow was on the square the morning Mrs. Hooper was killed and that he disappeared shortly thereafter. He hasn't been heard from since."

Worth noting when one considers the instinctive animosity he felt toward the deceased. I imagine the police are busily tracing his whereabouts. We'll leave Mr. Barlow to them for the moment. Anything else?

"Mrs. Hooper somehow got the vicar to let her take over Sally Pyne's job of dressing the baptismal font for Easter," I said. "Peggy Taxman thinks Sally's seething resentment might have led her to clout Pruneface in the head. Do you?"

I should think she'd murder the vicar rather than Mrs. Hooper, but I'm quibbling. Murders, my dear, are committed for all sorts of petty reasons. We mustn't discount Mrs. Taxman's opinions simply because she expresses them so frankly. Have you spoken with Mrs. Pyne?

"Not yet. Nicholas and I are going to meet up at the tearoom tomorrow morning and —" I stopped short as a query appeared on the page.

Nicholas?

"Nicholas Fox," I said. "Lilian Bunting's nephew, remember? He and I have decided to work together."

I asked you to enlist Emma Harris's help in making your inquiries.

"I know," I said, "but Emma's afraid that Kit will come unglued if she leaves him alone at the manor, so she's staying there to keep an eye on him."

Who will keep an eye on you?

I flushed.

Is Mr. Fox by any chance good-looking?

"Not in a classic way." It didn't seem

89

worth mentioning that a man didn't have to be classically handsome to be considered good-looking.

I see.

"He's a godsend," I stated firmly, and told Dimity about the Pyms' gingerbread. "I missed the point completely, but Nicholas caught on right away, and he had Peggy Taxman eating out of his hand at the grave site. He sees through people, Dimity, or he gets them to reveal themselves."

Am I to take it, then, that you feel no unseemly attraction to him?

"Not yet," I admitted, painfully aware of why Dimity thought it necessary to quiz me about Nicholas Fox. She knew me well enough to know that my track record was less than spotless when it came to remembering my wedding vows. I'd yet to do anything absolutely reprehensible, but there was no getting around the fact that I had what Aunt Dimity called "a wandering eye."

I'm glad to hear it. I trust Ruth and Louise's judgment, so I'd like you to continue making use of Mr. Fox — without making eyes at him.

I sank lower in the leather armchair, wishing I could resent her insinuations but knowing that I didn't have a leg to stand on.

"Bill will be home on Saturday," I reminded her.

Even better. The handwriting ceased briefly before continuing. *You mentioned a grave site. I presume you mean Mrs. Hooper's.*

"Yes." I sat up, happy to move on to another subject. "She was buried at Saint George's. That's where Nicholas and I spoke with Peggy Taxman."

Why was Mrs. Hooper buried in Finch? She has close relatives elsewhere, doesn't she?

"There's a son and a grandson," I said.

It seems odd that they would bury Mrs. Hooper in a place where she has no family. If I might suggest another line of inquiry . . . ?

"I'll see what I can find out," I promised, and felt nothing but relief when Aunt Dimity's handwriting faded from the page.

I wasn't prepared to answer any more questions about Nicholas Fox because I wasn't sure how I felt about him. He was smart and funny and genuinely kind, but he was also a bit intimidating. He was almost *too* good with people, *too* charming, and when he went into Zen listening mode, he was almost too observant. I didn't mind his seeing through other people, but I was slightly worried about what he'd see when he saw through me.

Sally Pyne had once aspired to transform her modest tearoom into a hokey themed oasis that would draw the tourist trade. Those aspirations had, to everyone's relief, faded over time, and the tearoom was again its humble self. Finch's tea-drinkers weren't fashionable or concerned with setting trends. They asked only for rich pastries, fresh scones, tasty sandwiches, and tea subtly infused with local gossip, in a setting that was homely and familiar.

Some of the tearoom's furnishings must have seemed overly familiar to its customers, since its Early Flea Market decor reflected Sally's passion for local auctions, car boot sales, and charity shops. A dozen mismatched tables were covered with tablecloths of widely varying patterns and set with an ever-changing display of crockery and utensils. The pictures on the walls ranged from sad clowns on velvet to a handful of splendid oils, and the sunburst clock above the cash register had once hung in the palatial dining room of a baronial hall. I loved the cozy, crazy chaos of the place and hoped that Sally would never again be tempted to mute it.

I pulled up in front of the tearoom just as Nicholas strode into the square from Saint George's Lane. He'd dressed in the dark brown trousers he'd worn the day we'd met, with a pale yellow cotton shirt beneath his brown tweed blazer. He carried his black trench coat over one arm in recognition of the threat posed by the gray clouds that were building overhead.

I waited for him at the slate sandwich board that stood outside the tearoom's front door. Sally jotted the day's special offerings on the slate, which was frequently washed clean by rain before her customers had a chance to read it.

"The first wave has departed," I told Nicholas as he approached. "We should have Sally mostly to ourselves for the next hour."

"Good," he said. "Let's hope she's in a chatty mood."

"If she's not, I'm sure you'll put her in one," I commented.

"I can but try." Nicholas opened the door and stood aside to let me enter first.

Sally Pyne was short and round and highly energetic. She'd already cleared the tables and reset them for the lunch crowd and was sitting at the table nearest the cash register, sampling one of her own excellent jam doughnuts, when we arrived. I motioned for her to stay seated while we joined her at the table, but she insisted on fetching a plateful of jam doughnuts and a pot of tea for two from the kitchen.

"Sally Pyne," I began when she'd resumed her seat, "may I introduce —"

"Nicholas Fox," she broke in, "the vicar's nephew. You two are thick as thieves these days. Bill out of town again?"

Aunt Dimity would, I thought, be delighted to hear how closely my neighbors were monitoring my behavior during my husband's absence. If I were ever foolish enough to have an affair, I decided, it would have to take place a long, long way from Finch.

While Sally demolished the jam doughnut, I presented her with the Pyms' gingerbread. It was a coals-to-Newcastle sort of gift for someone with Sally's baking skills, but she was impressed by the sisters' handiwork. They'd cut the cookies in four basic shapes — a cross, a paschal lamb, a palm frond, and a lily — and adorned them with intricate patterns of edible gold leaf.

After Sally had tucked the box of gingerbread behind the cash register, I carefully explained that my husband would be home on Saturday and that Lilian Bunting had asked me to entertain her nephew during his visit because the vicar wasn't feeling well.

Sally huffed triumphantly when she heard about the vicar. "He's probably worried sick about who's going to do the font for Easter. He knows better than to ask me."

"What a pity." Nicholas sounded truly disappointed. "I was so looking forward to seeing your arrangement, Mrs. Pyne. My aunt tells me that you're magical with moss."

"Vicar should've remembered that when he sacked me," Sally retorted.

"Indeed, he should have." Nicholas nodded gravely. "I believe he meant well when he reassigned the task to Mrs. Hooper. He was trying to make a new parishioner feel welcome."

"A new parishioner." Sally snorted derisively. "A bloodsucking piranha, more like. Vicar was bamboozled by Pruneface's smarmy flattery. She was sweet as honey when she saw something she wanted, and what she wanted was to *snub me.*"

Nicholas leaned forward. "Why on earth would she want to snub you?"

"Because I tossed her beastly grandson out of my tearoom." Sally pointed to a spot on the wall above the cash register, crying indignantly, "He broke my clock!"

I looked up and noticed for the first time that the glorious sunburst clock had been replaced by a cat-shaped plastic timepiece with hideous ticktocking eyes, a dial in its belly, and a swinging pendulum tail.

"Came in here with a football, the little beast, and threw it when I told him not to. Knocked my beautiful clock right off the wall," Sally went on. "I could've wrung his fat neck, but I just told him to get out. Next thing I know, Vicar's given the font to Pruneface." She paused to catch her breath. "Now, you may think I'm adding two plus two and getting five, but —"

"I don't," I interrupted. "Kit Smith had a run-in with Mrs. Hooper, involving her grandson, and she made him regret it."

Sally was all ears as I told her about the incident at the Anscombe Manor stables and the rumor Mrs. Hooper had spread to punish Kit for refusing to let her grandson ride Zephyrus.

Nicholas, on the other hand, was all eyes. I glanced at him a few times while recounting my tale and was mildly disconcerted by his sheer intensity. He'd gone into Zen listening mode, sitting absolutely motionless and watching Sally's face with an expression that was neither kindly nor good-humored. It was cold and hard and penetrating, as if he were recording Sally's minutest reactions for later in-depth analysis.

"I never did believe the folderol about Kit and Nell," Sally declared. "And even if it were true, where's the harm? Nell's older than her years, old enough to know her mind, and the man hasn't been born who could seduce her without her full cooperation. Besides, everyone knows that Kit's a saint. Nell could do a lot worse than fall in love with him." She pushed the plate of jam doughnuts toward us and urged us to partake. "It's Peggy Taxman who kept that rumor going about Kit seducing Nell, but I never did believe it. Parroting her chum, she was."

"Did you happen to mention the broken clock to the police?" Nicholas inquired.

"Why should I?" Sally demanded. "It had nothing to do with Pruneface's death. There's no need to tell the police every little thing that happens. It only clutters their minds."

Nicholas cocked his head to one side. "Mrs. Hooper seems to have been slightly neurotic about her grandson."

"She preferred her grandson to her son," Sally told him eagerly. "She treated that son of hers like dirt. Never heard her say a kind word to him without a razor buried in it, like ground glass folded into whipping cream, but that grandson of hers could do no wrong."

"Is that why she was buried in Finch," I asked, "instead of closer to her son?"

" 'Course it is," said Sally. "You could see it in the poor chap's eyes when he spoke at the wake. He was glad to see the back of her and didn't plan to haunt the graveyard like that deluded fleabrain Peggy Taxman."

"Mrs. Taxman seems to be the only person mourning Mrs. Hooper's death," Nicholas observed. "She's angry about it, too."

Sally rolled her eyes. "Peggy Taxman's been pointing fingers left and right ever since Pruneface was thumped. She thinks I did it because of the font, she thinks Kit did it to avoid more scandal, and I don't know why she thinks Billy Barlow did it but —"

"He was on the square that morning," Nicholas put in swiftly.

"He wasn't the only one," Sally pointed out, in full flow. "Dick Peacock was there, too, like he is every Thursday morning, keeping an eye out for —" She broke off abruptly, colored to the roots of her stylishly cropped white hair, and averted her gaze. "Good heavens, look at the time," she said, getting to her feet. "Have to get the kettles boiling before the lunch crowd tumbles in. Eat up, you two. I'll be back to top up your pot."

I lifted a jam doughnut from the plate. It wasn't like a doughnut in the States. Sally's jam doughnuts were made of heavy, chewy

98

dough. They were shaped like submarines, rolled in grainy sugar, split in two, and filled with thick, buttery whipped cream, with a scant dab of jam smeared down the middle. The mere sight of one made me weak with desire.

"I wonder," I said quietly, "if the scorned son stood to inherit anything from mommy dearest."

"That's the sort of thing the police will wonder, too, and they're better equipped than we are to look into it." Nicholas reached for a doughnut. "I'm more interested in finding out why Mr. Peacock's on the square every Thursday morning."

I felt a quiver of excitement. "Tomorrow's Thursday," I pointed out. "Do you want to mount a stakeout?"

"Why don't we try speaking with him first?" Nicholas's eyes widened as he bit into his doughnut. "My God," he mumbled reverently through a mouthful of heavy cream, "this is incredible."

"Don't eat more than one," I cautioned, glancing at the cat clock, "because in exactly twenty minutes we'll be sitting down to lunch at Peacock's pub."

Chapter 10

The heavens opened as soon as we left Sally's tearoom, so I decided to leave the Peacocks' gingerbread in the Rover for the time being. I pulled up the hood on my oiled-cotton jacket, Nicholas held his trench coat over his head like a cape, and we sprinted across the soggy green toward the pub.

Dick Peacock saw us coming and opened the door for us and a pair of field hands who'd dashed over from the Emporium. The experienced publican's ready greeting covered all four of us.

"Good weather for the crops," he remarked cheerfully as we shook the rain from our assorted coats, "but a dirty day to be on foot."

Dick Peacock was a large man, so big around that he'd been forced to widen the hatch in the bar to accommodate his girth. He was also finicky about his appearance. His mustache and goatee were works of art, and he had a closet full of brightly colored shirts. He'd chosen one in aquamarine today, perhaps in tribute to the "dirty" weather.

Dick's majestic proportions could be attributed directly to his wife's culinary skills. If Sally Pyne reigned supreme over all things rich and sweet, Christine Peacock was the rightful queen of grease. Christine's famous homemade sausages and chips came from the kitchen dripping, her fried bread and fried tomatoes glistened with globules of fat, and the crusts of her meat pies were laden with lard.

Christine was, as a result, nearly as big around as her husband, but she carried her weight gracefully and dressed to suit herself. As we hung our wet coats on the wall rack, she emerged from the pub's kitchen wearing a long-sleeved striped pullover and a pair of outsized jeans.

"Lori," she called. "Welcome home."

"Thanks," I replied. "It's good to be back."

While Dick served the field hands at the bar, Christine guided Nicholas and me to a table at the front window, talking nonstop.

"How was your visit to the States, Lori? And your father-in-law? He's well, I hope? And how are the boys? They must've grown a foot since I last saw them."

Christine's rapid-fire questions reached a

climax with an inquiry that had by now become as predictable as spring rain.

"Bill stayed on in London, did he?" Christine's blue eyes darted to Nicholas's face. "No trouble there, I hope."

"He's catching up on paperwork with his cousin Gerald," I explained patiently, "and he'll be home on Saturday. In the meantime, Lilian Bunting asked me to —"

"— show her nephew Nicholas round Finch." Christine turned to my companion. "I'm pleased to meet you, Nicholas. Dick saw you running by the river this morning. Gives a man an appetite, does running. Will you be having lunch?"

Christine's cholesterol-crammed cuisine may have been a cardiologist's nightmare, and it wasn't something I indulged in every day, but when I did, I invariably cleaned my plate. I ordered a classic fry-up, Nicholas followed my example, and Christine retreated to the kitchen.

"I didn't know you ran," I said to Nicholas.

"Penance for my gustatory sins," he confessed, "which have been mounting at an alarming rate ever since I arrived in Finch." He looked over at Dick Peacock and lowered his voice. "I suspect I'll have to run to Kathmandu and back to work off today's lunch."

I was still chuckling when Dick came to take our drinks order.

"I think the rain has scared away your regulars," I commented, eyeing the empty tables.

"It's a busy time of year for farming folk," Dick said. "They'll be in this evening, though, whatever the weather. Did I tell you how good it is to have you back, Lori? We missed you." He surveyed my smiling face, then extended his hand to Nicholas. "And you're the Buntings' nephew. Pleased to meet you, Nicholas. Lori seems to be having great fun with you. I haven't heard anyone laugh like that in ages."

"My aunt tells me that Finch hasn't had much to laugh about lately," Nicholas ventured. "Nasty business, a neighbor being murdered."

"Well, Nicholas, it depends on how you look at it." Dick stroked his goatee philosophically and gazed out of the window.

"I take your point." Nicholas nodded sagely, as if the publican had made a profound observation. "I suppose, for example, it could depend on how neighborly the neighbor was."

"That's it in a nutshell," Dick said. "And I'm sorry to say it, but Mrs. Hooper wasn't the neighborliest of neighbors."

"Is that right?" Nicholas looked puzzled. "Peggy Taxman told us that she took an interest in people. Surely that's an admirable quality."

"Well, Nicholas, it depends on how you look at it," Dick repeated. He folded his arms and settled back on his heels. "There's taking an interest, and there's poking your damned nose in places where it has no business being, and I'm sorry to say it, but old Pruneface had a snoot on her like a pachyderm." He smiled down at us beneficently. "Now, what will you be drinking?"

I ordered a half-pint of shandy, and Nicholas requested a pint of stout. When Dick had gone back to the bar, I raised both eyebrows.

"I've never heard Dick Peacock swear before," I murmured.

Nicholas leaned forward, whispering, "Pruneface the pachyderm strikes again."

An elephantine snort of laughter escaped me, and I turned my face to the window to hide my merriment. I didn't want to give Dick the impression that I was having *too* much fun with Nicholas.

"It's stopped raining," Nicholas observed, and sure enough, the cloudburst had ended, and the square had come to life. Little knots of people spilled out of the Emporium, the tearoom, and the greengrocer's and scattered in all directions. Most took advantage of the opportunity to make a dry escape and went directly to their cars.

"Huh," I said, catching sight of a lone figure walking from the tearoom toward Saint George's Lane. "There's George Wetherhead. We have a box of gingerbread for him." I watched the retired railwayman idly for a moment, then more attentively. There was something different about him, but I couldn't put my finger on what it was.

"Here you are." Dick Peacock had returned with our drinks. "Enjoy."

Nicholas took a long pull on his stout and wiped the froth from his mouth with the back of his hand. "A fine brew, Mr. Peacock."

"We aim to please," Dick said. His smile faltered slightly. "Not that you can please everyone. If that Hooper woman didn't like living next to a pub, she shouldn't have rented Crabtree Cottage."

"Indeed not," Nicholas agreed.

"There goes old George." Dick's smile returned as he noted the direction of my gaze. "He's looking awfully chipper these days, don't you think?"

"Where's his cane?" I asked suddenly. A hip injury suffered in a fall from a freight car had forced Mr. Wetherhead's early retirement from the railway. I'd never seen him walking without the aid of a three-pronged cane.

"Leaves it at home these days." Dick peered over his shoulder at the kitchen door, as if to make sure that his wife was safely out of earshot. When he turned back to us, he was smirking. "There's a spring in his step, wouldn't you say?"

"It's wonderful," I marveled. "What happened? Did he see another specialist?"

"In a manner of speaking," said Dick. "What I've heard about old George is —"

He fell into a guilty silence as his wife loomed at his elbow, carrying a serving tray. Grog, the Peacock's basset hound, trailed hopefully at her heels, his attention riveted on the artery-clogging, aromatic feast she placed before us.

Christine glared at her husband. "Did I hear you talking about Mr. Wetherhead?"

Dick raised a placating hand. "Now, dear, I was only trying to fill Lori in on the latest news."

"The latest nonsense, I'd call it." Christine planted one hand firmly on one broad hip. "It's nothing but rumors, Dick, and I won't have such talk repeated in my pub."

"Just because they're rumors doesn't

mean they aren't true," Dick said. "Where there's smoke —"

"— there's usually a large pile of rubbish," Christine broke in. "You'll do well to remember it, Richard Peacock. What folks get up to in their own home in the wee hours or at any other time is their business, so let that be an end to it."

Dick hastened to the bar in chastened silence, but the moment the kitchen door had swung shut behind his wife, he returned to our table, ostensibly to check the levels of our drinks.

I couldn't contain myself. "In the wee hours?" I prompted.

Dick's bearded face took on the avid expression of a devoted gossip. "Round about dawn, so I've heard."

"We've heard you're up at that hour," Nicholas murmured.

Dick's face froze for a fleeting second; then he laughed. "Me? Up at dawn? You ask Chris if I ever get up that early. She's lucky to roll me out of bed by opening time. But George, now, that's a different matter." He lowered his voice. "There's some who say you can't teach an old dog new tricks. But there's some tricks that'll put a spring in any old dog's step. Good for him, I say." His eyes narrowed. "But not so good for Mrs. Hooper.

107

She should've stayed out of old George's business." He pressed a finger to the side of his nose, then scurried back to the safety of the bar.

I caught a last glimpse of George Wetherhead as he entered Saint George's Lane. He wasn't striding like an athlete, but he was moving steadily and without the support of his cane. It was an incredible sight, though not half as incredible as Dick Peacock's sly insinuations.

I turned to Nicholas. "I can't believe —"

"Not now," he broke in quietly. "Mrs. Peacock's antennae are extended." He fed Grog a sliver of black pudding, and the basset hound gazed up at him worshipfully. "We'll take in the war memorial when we've finished lunch. Tell me then."

It was a case of hiding in plain sight. The war memorial stood at the north end of the green, in full view of the buildings on the square but far enough away from them to allow for confidential conversation.

As soon as Nicholas and I had cleared our greasy plates, we said good-bye to Chris and Dick and left the pub. We crossed the cobbled lane encircling the green and stood for a moment in the wet and spongy grass, as if debating what to do next. Nicholas motioned toward the imposing Celtic cross, and we strolled casually in its direction.

"We've established that Mrs. Hooper was vindictive," Nicholas began. "She held grudges on her grandson's behalf against both Mrs. Pyne and Kit, and she acted on those grudges in ways that infuriated each of them." He put a hand in the small of my back to guide me around a muddy puddle. "Now we're being told that she was intrusive as well."

"According to Dick, she poked her nose into George Wetherhead's business." I stepped around the wet patch, and Nicholas withdrew his guiding hand.

"To judge by Mr. Peacock's leer," he continued, "Mr. Wetherhead's business involves something naughty, something that's given him the strength to throw aside his cane and walk with a spring in his step." He stopped short. "Would it be fair to assume that Mrs. Hooper discovered what Mr. Wetherhead was doing and threatened to expose him?"

"It's fair," I said grimly. "I wouldn't put anything past Pruneface. On the other hand, I can't imagine George Wetherhead involved in something naughty. As far as I know, the only thing he gets up to in the wee hours is playing with his toy trains."

"Perhaps he's found a new hobby." Nicholas's suggestive smirk recalled Dick Peacock's.

I blinked in disbelief. "Like . . . an affair?"

"Sexual energy can work wonders on the anatomy." Nicholas gazed reflectively toward Saint George's Lane as we moved on. "I don't know if it can make the blind see, but it might make the lame walk."

The difficulties of conducting an illicit love affair in Finch had crossed my mind so recently that I didn't have to search for an objection.

"Mr. Wetherhead would have to be clinically insane to think he could keep an affair secret," I stated flatly. "Have you noticed how people keep shoving the word *husband* down my throat? You and I are already raising eyebrows, and we're only hanging out together."

Nicholas gave me a brief, diffident glance, then looked away. "Do you mind?"

"Being talked about?" The question took me off guard. I looked down at the rain-dappled grass and smiled shyly. "It's flattering, in a way. At least they haven't written me off as just another boring housewife."

"You will never be a boring housewife," Nicholas murmured. "No matter how hard you try." He opened his mouth as if he wanted to say more, then seemed to think better of it. "My point is," he resumed briskly, "that people engaged in passionate love affairs aren't necessarily thinking clearly. If Mr. Wetherhead's engaged in one, he might not pause to consider the consequences."

We'd reached the holly hedge Emma Harris had planted around the war memorial. Nicholas gazed up at the weathered cross, then stepped closer to it and bent low to read the names carved into its base.

My gaze wandered wonderingly to Saint George's Lane. It wasn't easy to envision short, balding, reserved Mr. Wetherhead in the throes of a passionate affair. He was so bashful that he rarely met my gaze in conversation and so modest that I could scarcely imagine him holding a woman's hand.

But perhaps my imagination was too limited. After all, George Wetherhead was human. Like the rest of us, he had needs, desires, dreams. If he'd found love, or a reasonable facsimile thereof, who was I to quibble? And who was Pruneface Hooper to go poking and prying into something that had nothing whatsoever to do with her?

"Okay." I leaned back against the cross and folded my arms. "*Maybe* Mr. Wetherhead is playing with something other than trains in the wee hours, and *maybe* Mrs. Hooper found out about it. I still can't believe that he killed her. He's the most inoffensive guy you'd ever want to meet."

"Haven't you heard? It's always the quiet ones who go spare." Nicholas ran his battered hand across the memorial's rough surface. "You have to face it, Lori. If Mrs. Hooper confronted Mr. Wetherhead with something he's deeply ashamed of, there's no telling how he might react."

"He's got strong arms, from using his cane," I acknowledged reluctantly. "I suppose he could have hit her hard enough to kill her."

"Irrelevant." Nicholas stood. "It wouldn't take a great deal of strength to inflict the kind of head wound that killed Mrs. Hooper."

"How do you know?" I asked.

"It came out at the inquest," Nicholas replied. "Mrs. Hooper was struck here" — he touched his fingertips lightly to the side of my head, froze, and jerked his hand away — "where the skull is particularly thin and vulnerable."

His touch sent a shiver through me, but I remained adamant. "If I stretch my imagination as far as it will go, I can almost conceive of him seeing some woman on the sly. But I can't stretch it any further. I can't see him as a murderer. I'm sure Dick Peacock's got the wrong end of the stick. Or . . ." I gave the pub a penetrating glance. "Or he's trying to direct suspicion away from himself. Sally Pyne says he's up early on Thursday mornings, but Dick claims to sleep in. Who's lying?"

"There's one way to find out," said Nicholas.

I straightened with alacrity. "Time for a stakeout?" I asked.

Nicholas's face softened as he looked down at me. "I do think it's time for a stakeout," he said, "but I don't think you should participate." He held up a hand to cut short my protest. "As you've pointed out, we're already raising eyebrows in the village. If we're seen sneaking about together at dawn, I'm afraid we'll start an avalanche of gossip."

"But —"

"Apart from that," Nicholas interrupted, "your Range Rover is far too conspicuous to use in a covert operation."

Much as I wanted to, I couldn't argue with his logic. My canary-yellow Range Rover stood out like a neon sign everywhere it went, and the rumor mill would kick into high gear if I were seen lurking at dawn with a man who was most definitely not my husband.

As he circumambulated the stone cross, I racked my brain to come up with a way to join the stakeout without jeopardizing it — or our reputations. The solution came to me so quickly that I nearly danced for joy.

"Bill's office," I said, scrambling after Nicholas. "It's right across from the pub. I go there all the time to fetch papers he's forgotten. I can go there just before dawn and sneak in through the back door. I'll be able to see everything that happens on the square."

"And everyone on the square will be able to see your Rover," Nicholas pointed out.

"I'll ride my bicycle!" I exclaimed, proud of my cleverness. "Everyone knows that Bill gave me a bike for Christmas and that I haven't had a chance to try it out yet. I'll take the road to the bridge, and from there I'll use the river path . . ." I began to outline my intended route with gestures, but Nicholas caught hold of my arm.

"Don't point," he scolded. "No need to give our plans away."

"*Our* plans?" I peered up at him anxiously. "You mean it?"

His smile brought light to the sunless day. "Four eyes, like four ears, are better than two." He tucked my hand into the crook of his arm, and we began to walk back to the

Rover. "While you watch the pub from your husband's office, I'll watch Mr. Wetherhead's house from the vicarage. We'll meet up later at your cottage to compare —" He broke off.

I felt him stiffen — his biceps bulged even through the triple layer of shirt, tweed blazer, and trench coat — as he came to an abrupt halt.

"What's wrong?" I asked.

"Nothing's wrong." He patted my hand, but his mind was clearly elsewhere. "It just struck me that there's only one place on the square from which one can view both the pub and Mr. Wetherhead's house simultaneously."

The hairs on the back of my neck prickled as we slowly turned to stare at Crabtree Cottage.

"Well, well, well," Nicholas murmured, half to himself. "What a perfectly splendid vantage point for spying on one's neighbors."

Chapter
11

Bill wasn't entirely happy when I told him of my plans to surveil the pub. By the time I'd finished recounting all that Nicholas and I had learned that day, he was very nearly vexed.

"It's not a game, Lori," he said repressively. "Prunella Hooper may have been killed because she saw something she shouldn't have seen. What if you see the same thing? What if you're found out? You could be putting yourself in danger."

"I'll lock the office door," I promised. "I'll keep well out of sight. No one will know I'm there." I clucked my tongue impatiently. "I'm glad that you're worried about me, Bill, but I honestly don't think it's necessary. Nicholas will take care of me." I tagged on the last sentence without pausing to consider the impression it might make.

It evidently made the wrong one.

There was a long pause before Bill asked, with excruciating nonchalance, "Will he?"

"He teaches self-defense," I said, carefully enunciating each word. "If any fool comes after me, Nicholas'll chop him up faster than my food processor." I sent up a silent prayer of thanks when Bill chuckled.

"I forgot about Nicholas's profession," he admitted, and finally agreed to telephone the cottage at three A.M. to add verisimilitude to my story of running into town to retrieve a file. "I should know by now that it's pointless to discourage you from taking risks," he added before we said good night. "I won't promise not to worry, love, but I'll rest easier knowing you have a bodyguard."

As I hung up the phone, I remembered the firm pressure of Nicholas's palm as he guided me around the muddy puddle by the war memorial. I felt safe when I was with him. If he wouldn't let me get my feet wet, he surely wouldn't let me come to more grievous bodily harm.

Aunt Dimity wasn't worried in the least about my safety.

I seriously doubt that Mrs. Hooper's murder was premeditated. The elegant lines of royal blue ink curled smoothly across the blue journal's blank page, reflecting Dimity's calm assessment of the situation. *A planned murder would have taken place in a back room or the shed, not in a window overlooking the square. No, I suspect it was a spur-of-the-moment, snap reaction to something regrettable Mrs. Hooper said or did. Our killer's not a professional, and he's not likely to strike again. He might even welcome your attention. He has a heavy burden on his conscience. It won't be lifted until he's brought to justice.*

"So you don't think I'll be in any danger," I confirmed.

The only danger you'll be in is catching cold if it rains tomorrow morning. Be sure to bundle up, my dear, and bring a change of clothing, just in case.

The motherly advice made me smile, but I couldn't shake the feeling Bill had engendered in me, that I might be biting off more than I could chew. Like a rabid animal, Mrs. Hooper had poisoned everyone with whom she'd come in contact. She'd forced Kit to find his temper, brought a curse to Dick Peacock's lips, and left Sally Pyne embittered enough to gloat over the vicar's ill health. I knew Kit would never turn on me, but how could I be sure about the others? As I returned Aunt Dimity's journal to its niche on the shelves, I decided to call upon an old friend for moral support.

"Reginald," I said. I took the pink-flannel rabbit down from the shelf and ran a fingertip along his hand-stitched whiskers.

"You and I have been through the wars together. How'd you like to join me on a stakeout?"

I hadn't ridden a bicycle in ten years, and I'd never ridden one in a monsoon. The fact that it was pitch-dark when I left the cottage made the ride into the village even less of a treat. The bicycle's headlamp illuminated about two square inches of the road ahead, but I couldn't see even those two inches clearly because of the rain sluicing my face.

I'd worn the all-weather jacket and pants Bill had included with his Christmas present, but icy, wind-lashed droplets kept finding chinks in my rainproof armor. By the time I reached the humpbacked bridge, my turtleneck and jeans were uncomfortably damp, my hands were numb, and I was feeling far less clever than I had the day before. When I thought of Nicholas keeping watch over George Wetherhead's house from the cozy confines of the vicarage, I wanted to spit.

I dismounted at the bridge, switched off the headlamp, and walked the bike along the river path that wound behind the buildings on the east side of the square. Three miles of vigorous pedaling had left me hobbling almost as gingerly as my ride on Zephyrus had done, which made negotiating the slippery path a challenge. I groaned with relief when I made it to the back door of Wysteria Lodge, the picturesque house that had become Bill's place of business.

Panic threatened when my frigid fingers fumbled for the key, but I found it eventually, in the outside pocket of the daypack into which I'd also tucked a change of clothes, per Dimity's sage advice, and Reginald. I leaned the bicycle against the wall and let myself into the office's windowless back storage room.

I paused to wipe my face and rub my sore behind before reaching for the light switch on the wall. I clicked it several times, but nothing happened. With a stifled grumble of frustration, I groped for the box of candles Bill kept on hand for just such emergencies. Power outages during inclement weather were not unknown in Finch.

I changed by candlelight into black wool trousers and a ruby-red chenille sweater, blew the candle out, and opened the door to the main office, where I felt my way past the photocopier, the fax machine, the printer stand, the file cabinets, and the myriad other obstacles that stood between me and the front window. I longed for a nice hot cup of tea but the electric kettle wouldn't work without electricity, so I huddled at the window, hugging Reginald for warmth and wishing he were Nicholas instead.

The idle thought startled me, and I thrust it aside, but as the minutes ticked by it returned, demanding my attention so forcibly that I finally gave myself up to it.

It was useless to deny the flicker of attraction that I felt for Nicholas, and Bill's absence didn't make things any easier. For the first time it occurred to me that I was lucky to have a host of nosy watchdogs standing guard over my marriage, since I was so transparently ill equipped to manage on my own. Did every marriage require community support? I wondered wistfully. Maybe not, but mine evidently did, not because of any failure on Bill's part but because of my own abiding weakness for charming men.

My troubled meditations were interrupted by a rush of adrenaline as the pub's front door opened and Dick Peacock appeared, draped in a massive rainproof poncho. It was one minute past five o'clock. The merest wisps of thin gray daylight had begun to smudge the square, and Dick, in his black poncho, looked as huge and as forbidding as a storm cloud.

He glanced once at his wristwatch, then let his gaze traverse the square. Reginald and I ducked when he looked in our direction, and I counted to ten before I raised our heads again. Dick was staring up Saint George's Lane and shifting restlessly from foot to foot.

My pulse raced when I heard the faint sound of a vehicle changing gears. A moment later, a gray van emerged from the lane and stopped at the pub. Dick opened the van's rear door, and he and the driver began unloading cardboard boxes, which they carried into the pub. They worked methodically, with the speed and efficiency of a well-practiced team.

The boxes appeared to be unmarked and fairly heavy. The men unloaded three each before Dick closed the rear door, handed a small white packet — an envelope? — to the driver, and hurried back into the pub. The driver tucked the packet inside his slicker, hopped into the driver's seat, and drove around the square. Reginald and I hunkered down again as he passed Wysteria Lodge, but I scribbled the license-plate number on a scrap of paper before the van vanished up Saint George's Lane.

That was it. The drama was over. The rain continued falling, the sun rose bit by bit, and the buildings on the square seemed once again as devoid of life as the churchyard's weathered tombs.

I sat back on my heels and gazed thoughtfully into Reginald's black button eyes.

"Contraband," I murmured. "What do you think, Reg? Is Dick Peacock smuggling liquor into Finch? Does Sally Pyne know about it? More important still, did Mrs. Hooper —" I fell silent as a cold draft of air wafted over me.

Someone had opened the back door.

I clutched Reginald to my breast and crept behind Bill's desk, peering fearfully toward the storage room. I was reaching for the telephone when I heard a soft thump and a muffled "Ow!"

"Nicholas?" I whispered, and hastened in a half-crouch to the storeroom.

His quiet voice floated to me from the darkness. "Yes, Lori, it's Nicholas."

"Stay where you are." I closed the door behind me and relit the squat white candle I'd left standing on a box of files.

Nicholas stood just inside the back door, rubbing the knee he'd bashed against a plastic storage bin. He was wearing a rain-proof windbreaker, but his pant legs were damp, his shoes muddy, and his hair hung in draggled tresses he'd pushed behind ears he had no reason to hide. His sea-green eyes by candlelight took my breath away.

"You're wet," I said, trying valiantly to ignore my galloping heart. "I think Bill has some towels somewhere."

"Don't bother," he murmured, straightening. "I'm fine."

"You're not fine," I insisted, rummaging for the towels. "You're wet and muddy and —"

"I'm fine," he repeated. "There's no need to fuss."

"I'm not fussing. I'm . . ." I stopped my search and commanded my treacherous heart to behave itself. "What are you doing here, Nicholas? I thought we agreed —"

He stepped closer to me. "I know what we agreed, but I couldn't wait." He came closer still, so close that I could feel his warm breath on my skin. "Is that . . . a rabbit you're holding?"

I looked down at my pink-flannel chaperon, mortified. I started to explain that I'd been nervous and in need of moral support, but soon gave up and bowed my head, murmuring morosely, "It's not something you would understand."

"I understand what it is to be alone and afraid during a stakeout," Nicholas said softly. He lifted my chin with his fingertips. "It was wise of you to bring a talisman."

It took every ounce of willpower I possessed to keep myself from reaching up to smooth away the scattered raindrops sparkling like tears on Nicholas's face. If Reginald hadn't been there, I might have smoothed them away with my lips.

"W-what couldn't wait?" I managed, shoving my free hand firmly into my trouser pocket.

His fingers lingered briefly beneath my chin, then fell away. "George Wetherhead is with a woman," he whispered. "She was wearing a hooded cape when she entered his house, so I couldn't see her clearly, but I'm certain that you'll know who she is."

"Why?" I asked.

"Because," he said, his bright eyes dancing, "she lives across the street from my aunt and uncle."

My brain seized for a moment. "M-Miranda Morrow?" I sputtered. "George Wetherhead is having an affair with *Finch's witch?*"

Chapter 12

Miranda Morrow was a tall and shapely strawberry blonde in her mid-thirties who practiced telephone witchcraft for a living. She had a flat in London but spent a good part of the year at Briar Cottage, which stood directly across Saint George's Lane from the vicarage.

Mr. Wetherhead, by contrast, was a short and balding man in his mid-fifties who ran a train museum to augment his disability pension. He never went to London; in truth, he spent so much of his time creating miniature landscapes for his toy trains that he seldom left his home, which stood between the old schoolhouse and the vicarage.

"Miranda Morrow and George Wetherhead?" My mind reeled. "I don't believe it."

"Then come and see for yourself," Nicholas coaxed. "If we hurry, we may catch her as she's leaving."

I grabbed my jacket and threw caution to the wind. The rumor mill would grind itself into dust if Nicholas and I were seen together, but I couldn't pass up the chance to find out for myself if Finch had spawned the most improbable pair of lovers in the history of affection.

Reginald, however, remained behind. I didn't want the added burden of the daypack, and with Nicholas at my side, I feared no one.

Nicholas extinguished the candle and led the way through the back door. From that point on, it was all I could do to keep up with him. I'd assumed we'd take the river path to George Wetherhead's house, but Nicholas had reconnoitered a more direct route. The fact that his shortcut involved hopping walls, ducking branches, and squeezing through a hedgerow didn't bother him. He moved as lithely as a panther and used simple hand gestures to signal changes in speed and direction.

I scampered after him as swiftly as I could, the rain and my sore muscles forgotten in the exhilaration of the chase. I felt as if I were flying.

We slowed when we reached the old schoolhouse, then crept stealthily to the far corner of the schoolyard wall. George Wetherhead's house stood not ten yards from us, its windows shrouded with heavy drapes.

We worked our way along the wall until we had an unobstructed view of the front door, but Nicholas wasn't content to watch from a distance. He darted forward and moved from window to window, searching for a gap in the curtains.

I was appalled. I had no intention of playing Peeping Tom, and I didn't think Nicholas should, either. When he motioned for me to join him near a side window, I went forward to express my displeasure.

I'd just tweaked the sleeve of his windbreaker when I heard the sound of Miranda Morrow's fruity voice coming from inside the house.

"Six o'clock, darling. Time for me to go. If you'll take up your trousers . . . I think you've had enough for one morning, don't you?"

I recoiled, grabbed Nicholas's arm, and yanked him away from the window. I shook my head vehemently to indicate that his days as a voyeur were over, and we retreated to the back of the house. Having identified Miranda's inimitable voice, I no longer needed to watch the front door for her departure.

Nicholas slipped nimbly over the wall that separated George Wetherhead's back garden from the Buntings' and made for the French doors that gave access to the vicar's study. I clambered over the wall less gracefully, landed up to my ankles in what appeared to be a small lake, and remembered too late that I'd used up my allotment of dry clothing. With a heavy sigh, I waded ashore and followed Nicholas up the stone steps to the glass-paned doors.

Bill and I had spent many a pleasant evening in the book-lined study at the rear of the vicarage. Its furnishings were as shabby — and as comfortable — as an old bathrobe, but they didn't deserve to be treated shabbily. I wrung out my puddle-soaked trouser cuffs and took off my sopping sneakers before entering the room.

By the time I came inside, Nicholas had kicked off his shoes, peeled off his windbreaker, lit a fire in the fireplace, and retrieved a pair of cotton towels as well as a woolen blanket from his aunt's linen closet. He placed my sneakers beside his shoes near the fire and nodded toward the green velvet sofa that faced the vicar's armchair across the hearth.

"Have a seat," he said. "You must be chilled to the bone."

"There's no need to fuss." I sat on the sofa and held my hand out for a towel. "I'm *fine*."

Nicholas smiled wryly as he wrapped the

woolen blanket around my shoulders. We spent a moment in companionable silence, toweling our hair while the fire leapt and crackled and warmed the room. When my short curls and his long locks were sufficiently blotted, Nicholas took the damp towels away and returned with two large mugs of hot cocoa. He presented one to me, sat in the vicar's armchair, and held his stockinged feet out to the fire.

I swung my legs up on the couch, to put my own feet within drying distance of the flames, and eyed Nicholas speculatively as I sipped the steaming cocoa.

"You should be ashamed of yourself," I said. "What did you think you were doing, looking in on them like that?"

"I was confirming a hunch," he replied.

"What hunch?" I asked.

"One of recent vintage. It came to me when you mentioned Ms. Morrow's profession." He peered at me quizzically over the rim of his mug. "What do you think they were doing back there?"

"It seemed pretty clear to me," I mumbled, blushing.

"You didn't even look," he objected.

"I didn't *want* to look," I retorted.

Nicholas shook an index finger at me. "Never theorize in advance of the facts,

Lori. It's fatal to any investigation."

"Okay, Chief Inspector," I said sarcastically. "Tell me what you saw."

"I saw" — Nicholas paused for dramatic effect, then went on matter-of-factly — "a skilled physiotherapist ministering to a patient."

My mouth fell open, and Nicholas grinned.

"I saw Ms. Morrow administering a therapeutic massage to Mr. Wetherhead," he clarified. "Her manner was that of a highly competent and professional therapist. She was using a portable massage table and a kit stocked with what I assume to be herbal oils of her own devising." He finished his cocoa and set the mug aside. "Witchcraft is, among other things, a healing profession."

"A therapeutic massage," I repeated, as whole piggy banks of pennies began to drop. "Miranda's been working on George's injured hip. That's why he doesn't need a cane anymore."

"It may also explain the clandestine nature of her visits," Nicholas said. "A hip injury would require manipulations of fairly intimate parts of the anatomy. Mr. Wetherhead might permit them to ease his suffering, but he might at the same time find them rather embarrassing."

"He would," I stated firmly. "Especially

since it's a woman doing the manipulating, and not just any woman, but an attractive, unmarried witch. The poor guy . . ." I cupped the mug between my hands. "He was so afraid of scandal that he scheduled his treatments in a way that sparked the very rumors he was afraid of." I finished my cocoa and placed the mug on the small table at the head of the couch. "Dick Peacock's going to be sadly disappointed when the truth comes out."

"Speaking of Mr. Peacock . . . ," Nicholas prompted.

I told him about the van, the cardboard boxes, and the packet Dick had given to the driver. I was proud of myself for remembering the van's plate number without referring to my scribbled note.

"Mrs. Pyne was telling the truth," said Nicholas, "and Mr. Peacock was concealing it."

"I think he's buying smuggled liquor," I said.

"It's possible." Nicholas wriggled his toes as if savoring the fire's warmth. "It's not easy to keep a pub going in a place as small as Finch. Mr. Peacock wouldn't be the first landlord to cut costs by stocking his bar with tax-free brew."

"Sally Pyne seems to know what he's doing," I pointed out, "and she doesn't seem to mind. Pruneface, on the other hand, may not have been so tolerant."

Nicholas tilted his head back and recited, "There's taking an interest and there's poking your damned nose in places where it has no business being." He pursed his lips. "Mrs. Hooper seems to have poked her nose into Mr. Peacock's business as well as Mr. Wetherhead's."

"She probably spied on both of them from Crabtree Cottage." I curled my legs under me, drew the blanket over my lap, and leaned back against the sofa's velvet arm. "I wonder if she threatened to expose them?"

"If she did," said Nicholas, "it would give both men a motive for murder. Her wagging tongue would have threatened Mr. Peacock's livelihood and Mr. Wetherhead's health."

I gazed unhappily into the fire. Aunt Dimity believed that the murder had been a spur-of-the-moment reaction to something regrettable Mrs. Hooper had said or done. Threatening one's neighbors was nothing if not regrettable. Had one of the men snapped? Dick Peacock was as strong as he was large. A glancing blow from him would be enough to crack Prunella Hooper's skull.

And George Wetherhead's three-pronged cane was an undeniably blunt instrument.

I glanced over at Nicholas. He was staring at the dancing flames and slowly combing his fingers through his hair. The vagrant gold strands gleamed in the firelight, and his eyes shone like liquid opals.

"Doesn't it get in the way?" I asked.

He came out of his reverie. "Sorry?"

"Your hair," I said. "Doesn't it get in the way when you're karate-chopping people?"

"Perfect vision isn't essential if one hones one's other senses." He sat forward in his chair. "Close your eyes."

I closed them.

"Listen," he instructed, "not with your ears alone but with your entire body. Try to locate me."

I cheated at first and focused on my sense of hearing, but Nicholas in stockinged feet on a Turkish carpet, however threadbare, made not a sound.

I closed my eyes more tightly and widened my focus until I felt as if I were listening with my skin. This time I felt a tingle, as if an electrical field surrounding me had been subtly altered. I raised my hand, reached out, and seemed to touch spun silk. I opened my eyes to find my fingers tangled in Nicholas's hair.

He was on his knees beside me. He gazed at me in silence for a moment, then brought his shadowed face so close to mine that I caught the scents of wood smoke and rain lingering on his skin.

"Your sixth sense can alert you to many things," he said softly. "Not only physical sensation but emotion, intention . . . It can help you to avoid danger if you trust it."

We were alone in the study. No nosy neighbors were keeping watch, and Reginald was in Wysteria Lodge. I let my fingers trail through his hair.

Nicholas caught his breath and gathered my hand in his, murmuring, "Not a good idea."

"Sorry," I said, but made no attempt to withdraw my hand.

"Don't apologize," he said. "It's been hovering in the air for a while. We may as well admit it." He ran his thumb along the back of my hand and lightly stroked each finger. "I won't deny that I'm drawn to you, Lori, but we have to leave it there. Anything else would be too . . . complicated. For you. Not only because you're married, but because you live here. This is your home. I'm merely passing through."

"Right." A wave of regret tumbled through me and I ducked my head to hide my confusion. Nicholas was talking common sense. I was the one with my head in the clouds.

He released my hand and sat back on his heels. "There's a palpable charge between us, Lori. It crackles every time our eyes meet. What are we going to do about it?"

"Ground it," I said unsteadily, "and move on."

"I hope we can, because we've serious work ahead of us" — his fingertips grazed my cheek — "and I'm not beyond temptation."

The floorboards in the hallway creaked, and Lilian Bunting entered the study, clad in bedroom slippers and a quilted dressing gown. She looked from me, reclining on the sofa beneath a rumpled blanket, to Nicholas, kneeling closely by my side, and raised an inquisitive eyebrow.

"I could ask if you've been here all night," she said, "but I'm not sure I want to know the answer."

"Then offer us breakfast instead," Nicholas suggested. "We've been sleuthing since dawn and we're famished."

"Sleuthing?" Lilian pursed her lips as if intending to keep her thoughts to herself, but as she turned to leave the room she murmured audibly, "I sincerely hope that's *all* you've been doing since dawn."

Chapter 13

Lilian and the vicar listened somberly as we described what the dawn's early light had revealed. Nicholas did most of the talking. I was too busy stuffing my face with toast, marmalade, sausages, and poached eggs. My early-morning workout had sharpened my appetite, but I felt astonishingly alert and eager to get on with the investigation.

I'd telephoned Annelise to let her know where I was and that I might be gone longer than I'd planned. When she offered to bring me a change of clothes, I told her not to bother. My sneakers and puddle-dampened trousers had dried nicely before the fire in the study.

"It seems we were sadly mistaken about Mrs. Hooper," admitted Lilian when Nicholas had finished summarizing our suspicions.

The vicar's already-pensive expression became more pensive still. "I thought she was merely being helpful when in fact she was using me in her petty vendetta against Sally Pyne." He frowned thoughtfully. "She never criticized Sally's floral arrangements overtly, you understand. It was the way she admired them, always with a slight droop of disappointment in her voice, as if the bouquets weren't quite up to snuff."

"Sally said she never gave a compliment without implying a criticism," I interjected. "Like ground glass folded into whipping cream."

"In retrospect, I concede it to be an apt description." The vicar folded his hands and rested them on the table. "I was a fool to be taken in by her."

"As was I," Lilian said loyally.

"Don't blame yourselves," I told them. "Kit and Sally both said that Mrs. Hooper could be extraordinarily charming when she put her mind to it."

"She could also be extraordinarily vindictive," Nicholas added. "She sought to avenge supposed wrongs done to her grandson by ruining Kit's reputation and stealing Sally Pyne's thunder. Has Mr. Wetherhead had a run-in with the boy?"

"I doubt it," said the vicar. "George avoids confrontation whenever possible."

"She was rather prudish," Lilian offered. "She was quite shocked when I told her the story about the old schoolmaster's personal involvement in increasing the school's population. She thought it reflected badly on the village. If she believed that George was misbehaving with Miranda, she might have felt a moral obligation to step in."

"God save us from self-righteous busy-bodies," the vicar murmured.

Nicholas dipped a triangle of toast into the yolk of his poached egg. "What about Mr. Peacock? What did Mrs. Hooper stand to gain from harassing Finch's favorite publican?"

"She was a teetotaler," Lilian said promptly. "She never missed our sherry evenings, but she refused to drink anything stronger than tea. I must say that she made the rest of us feel rather louche, in an unspoken, terribly polite sort of way."

"More ground glass," I mumbled through a mouthful of marmalade-slathered toast.

"If that's the case, why in God's name did she choose to live beside Peacock's pub?" the vicar expostulated. "Crabtree Cottage can't have been much of a bargain, not with Peggy Taxman collecting the rent."

"They were old friends," Lilian reminded him. "Perhaps Peggy gave Mrs. Hooper a special rate."

The vicar looked skeptical but allowed

that there was a first time for everything.

"Let's not get sidetracked," I said. I put my fork down and focused on the matter at hand. "Let's say that Mrs. Hooper was a crusading prohibitionist as well as a prude, a snoop, and a liar. If she saw Dick Peacock receiving smuggled liquor, she'd have all the ammunition she'd need to shut him down."

"And Mr. Peacock," said Nicholas, "would have a good reason to want her dead."

His observation seemed to cast a pall over the Buntings. The vicar studied his fingernails, and Lilian shook her head sorrowfully. When Nicholas opened his mouth to speak, I motioned for him to concentrate on his breakfast instead. His aunt and uncle needed time to digest what they'd learned about a woman they'd once admired.

The vicar pushed his chair back from the table, stood, and walked to the window to peer out at Saint George's Lane.

"The village has been rippling with undercurrents for months," he said heavily. "I sensed bitterness, furtiveness, guilt, but I paid them little heed. I thought Sally Pyne would return to church when her wounded pride had healed. I rejoiced to see George Wetherhead's improved health without once asking how it came about."

Lilian nodded. "I heard vague rumors

about Kit and dismissed them out of hand, but I never thought to demonstrate my support publicly. And it never occurred to me that financial difficulties might force Dick Peacock to engage in illegal activities. I was under the impression that the pub was flourishing."

"We've been woefully inattentive shepherds," the vicar concluded. "Is it any wonder that one of our flock has gone astray?"

"Aunt Lilian, Uncle Teddy," Nicholas said, "we don't know if anyone has strayed so far as to commit murder. Lori and I have done nothing more than gathered scraps of local gossip."

"You need to gather facts," Lilian said firmly. "Dick Peacock has some explaining to do, as does George Wetherhead. You must give each man a chance to explain where he was when Mrs. Hooper died."

The vicar concurred. "Perhaps Miss Morrow will be able to provide Mr. Wetherhead with an alibi." He reached up to massage his right shoulder. "I wonder if she would bring her skills to bear on my bursitis?"

"It seems unlikely that the bishop will approve of any treatment given by a pagan," Lilian pointed out.

"Oh, I don't know," the vicar temporized. "We're very ecumenical these days." He stopped rubbing his shoulder and waved his hand in the direction of the square. "Speak of the — Well, we don't know that he's a devil, but I hope the two of you will soon find out." He swung about to look at me and Nicholas. "George Wetherhead has returned from the Emporium with his daily loaf. I believe I hear the sound of opportunity knocking."

Nicholas and I exchanged dubious glances.

"Vicar," I said patiently, "what do you think will happen when your nephew and I show up out of the blue, asking Mr. Wetherhead to explain something he's been trying to hide for who-knows-how-many months?"

"He'll slam the door on us," said Nicholas.

"Even if we do get a foot in the door, we'll have to use dynamite to open his mouth." I lifted my fork and speared one last succulent bite of sausage. "The Pyms' gingerbread would've given us a plausible excuse to drop in on him, but I didn't bring his box with me this morning."

"Take a box of my lemon bars instead," Lilian suggested. "I baked a batch last night, and I know that Mr. Wetherhead's inordinately fond of them."

"Whatever you do, please make haste," the vicar urged. "The suspense is making me dyspeptic."

Mr. Wetherhead's home was every bit as humble as its owner. The one-story dwelling was built of golden stone and sat well back from the lane amid a garden that was little more than a patch of balding lawn. It was as if the retired railwayman lavished so much attention on the minuscule landscapes he created for his model trains that he had none to spare for the full-size landscape surrounding his house.

He seemed somewhat dismayed to find Nicholas and me standing on his doorstep on such a rainy morning. He fidgeted with the collar of his plaid shirt, mumbled a response to my greeting, and plunged his hands into the pockets of his corduroy trousers before looking up at Nicholas.

"You're the nephew," he said bluntly. "If you're collecting for the church, you can tell your uncle that I give generously every Sunday."

His boldness surprised me. The George Wetherhead I knew would have given his last tuppence to the church rather than make a fuss. Miranda's treatments had evidently strengthened his mind as well as his body.

"We're not collecting anything," I assured him, and held up the cardboard box Lilian had filled with her tangy-sweet confections. "We've come to give you something."

"What's that?" he said, eyeing the box suspiciously.

"Aunt Lilian made lemon bars last night," said Nicholas. "She wondered if you might —"

"Lemon bars?" Mr. Wetherhead seemed to relax. "I thought you were going to land me with a load of the Pyms' rubbishy gingerbread, the way you've done everyone else. Never could stand the stuff. But lemon bars, that's different."

I could almost hear his mouth watering, so I decided to strike while the iron was steaming. "Would it be too much trouble to show Nicholas your trains as long as we're here?"

"Oh, yes, please," Nicholas chimed in. "I'd love to see your trains. Lori's told me so much about them."

"I suppose . . . Yes, alright." Mr. Wetherhead acquiesced grudgingly after I handed over the box of lemon bars. "Museum's not open till May, but I suppose I can make an exception for the vicar's nephew. . . ."

I'd seen grown men regress instantly to childhood upon entering Mr. Wetherhead's

144

humble abode. He'd furnished the front room with a series of plywood sheets on saw-horses, upon which he'd built an astonishingly detailed miniature mountain range. The snowy peaks and verdant valleys were so realistically rendered that I half-expected tiny trout to leap from the sparkling river. Precisely laid ribbons of train tracks wound from one Alpine village to the next, traversed fields, farms, and forests, and crossed the shining river on a cunningly constructed trestle bridge.

The prodigious display of craftsmanship rendered me speechless, but Nicholas wasn't quite so overwhelmed. He said the right things, and said them in a properly awestruck tone of voice, but as he spoke, his searching gaze moved past the mini-Matterhorn to the closed door at the far end of the room.

"Aunt Lilian tells me you've a notable collection of railroad memorabilia," he said, stepping toward the door. "Is it through here?"

"The memorabilia room is closed to the public," Mr. Wetherhead announced.

"Come, now, Mr. Wetherhead," Nicholas chided, still edging toward the door. "Lori's not the public. She's an old friend, and I hope you'll come to regard me as —"

"Here, you, stop!" shouted Mr. Wetherhead, but though he was more agile than he'd once been, he still wasn't quick enough to keep Nicholas from breezing into the next room without a backward glance.

Mr. Wetherhead hobbled after him in high dudgeon, and I took up the rear. As I entered the darkened room, I caught a tell-tale gleam of light from the small gap in the heavy draperies covering the window where Nicholas had played Peeping Tom.

The memorabilia room had been tidied since I'd last seen it. The helter-skelter accumulation of station signs, signal lanterns, and timetables had been organized by category and neatly labeled. The most noticeable difference in the room, however, was the floor space that had been cleared around Miranda Morrow's portable massage table.

Nicholas strode directly to the table. "What a curiously modern artifact," he mused aloud. "Was it used by the train crew or the passengers, I wonder?"

"It's none of your business," barked Mr. Wetherhead.

"You're quite right, sir. It isn't." Nicholas faced the infuriated little man. "But I wish you'd confide in me before the police ask you to confide in them."

"The p-police?" Mr. Wetherhead paled.

"What are you talking about?"

"I'm talking about murder." Nicholas stood motionless. In the dim half-light, he looked almost menacing. "It's not a nice subject, but it's one I think you know something about, something you haven't told the police."

Mr. Wetherhead blinked nervously. "I t-told them the t-truth," he stammered.

"I'm sure you did," crooned Nicholas, placing a hand on the massage table, "but did you tell them the whole truth or only part of it?"

Mr. Wetherhead's gaze was drawn inexorably to the table. His cheek twitched, and beads of perspiration appeared on his dome-like forehead. "I . . . I . . ."

"Who are you protecting?" Nicholas pressed in a voice as soft as velvet. "Yourself or Ms. Morrow?"

"I'm not . . . I'm . . ." Mr. Wetherhead lifted his chin defiantly. "If you try to lay the blame on Miranda, I'll say that she was with me when that woman died."

"You'll *say* she was with you?" Nicholas's velvet voice became a battering ram. "But that's not true. That's not even partly true. Your lies may have worked with the police, sir, but they won't work with me because *I know what you've been up to.* I know that Ms.

Morrow leaves here at six A.M., and I know that Mrs. Hooper died between five and nine." Nicholas struck the table with a clenched fist. "*Tell me the truth,* sir, or —"

"Miranda should get a medal for killing Pruneface!" cried Mr. Wetherhead. "The evil-minded cow deserved to die!"

Chapter 14

The silence that filled the room was broken only by the sound of lemon bars rattling in the cardboard box. Mr. Wetherhead was shaking so badly that I feared his legs would give way beneath him. I shot a reproachful glance at Nicholas and took the little man gently by the elbow.

"Come on, George," I said, guiding him toward the kitchen. "I'll put the kettle on."

Mr. Wetherhead wasn't the only one shaken by Nicholas's performance. I was as rattled as the lemon bars. The brow-beating bully who'd surfaced in the memorabilia room bore little resemblance to the soft-spoken, kindly man who'd wrapped a blanket around my shoulders in the vicar's study. I understood why Nicholas had employed such harsh tactics, and I was glad of the results, but the confrontation had made me uncomfortably aware that my newfound friend could be as ruthless as he was charming.

He turned on the charm when we reached the kitchen. While I made tea, he sat across from Mr. Wetherhead at the Formica-topped kitchen table and offered a sincere apology for his behavior.

Mr. Wetherhead wasn't mollified. "You're no different from her," he mumbled, wiping the sweat from his brow. "Come here all sweetness and light, pretending to tell me things for my own good. Being neighborly, she called it — pah! You're exactly like her."

"We're not like Mrs. Hooper." I placed the sugar bowl and the cream jug on the table and transferred the lemon bars from the box to a serving dish. "She wanted to make trouble. We want to clear it up."

"Clear it up?" Mr. Wetherhead moaned. "How can you clear it up?"

"By discovering the truth," Nicholas answered. "That's what we're trying to do, and we can't do it without your help."

Nicholas said nothing more until I'd taken my place at the table and poured the tea. The pause, the tea, and a large bite of lemon bar seemed to restore Mr. Wetherhead's composure. When Nicholas spoke again, the little man was no longer shaking.

"We know why Miranda Morrow has been coming to see you," Nicholas told him. "We know that she's been acting as your physiotherapist. Why don't we start there?"

"It was Miranda's idea." Mr. Wetherhead gave a small moan and sipped his tea. "She'd done a course in rehabilitative therapy, you see. She was convinced that therapeutic massage combined with regular doses of her herbal medicines would ease the stiffness in my joints. . . ."

The whole story came out in short order, and it was much as I'd imagined it would be. Mr. Wetherhead had been tempted by the prospect of improved mobility but embarrassed by the hands-on nature of the treatment. When he'd proposed conducting sessions at an early hour, to ensure privacy, Miranda Morrow had agreed to give it a try.

"I wanted to protect her reputation," Mr. Wetherhead explained. "You know how people talk in Finch if they think someone's fooling around. The things I've heard about you two would curl your —" He looked from my tousled curls to Nicholas's cascading waves and ducked his head. "Well, anyway, it'd make you blush."

A smile tugged at the corner of Nicholas's mouth, but he mastered it and asked soberly, "Did Mrs. Hooper suspect you and Ms. Morrow of fooling around?"

Mr. Wetherhead's face twisted into an indignant frown. "She stood there in that window of hers and looked down on the rest of us like she was some sort of holy saint. Came here to shake her finger at me and tell me to stop philandering or —" The words seemed to catch in his throat. He broke off abruptly and took a long pull on his cup of tea.

Nicholas waited until Mr. Wetherhead had slaked his thirst before murmuring sympathetically, "I do realize how difficult this must be for you. Would it help if I told you that nine times out of ten your worst fears don't come true? You may think you know what happened to Mrs. Hooper, but you may be wrong."

"I could be wrong," Mr. Wetherhead said, as if the idea hadn't occurred to him before. "I didn't actually see who smashed her head in."

Nicholas flinched, but his voice was soothing. "Of course you didn't. But Mrs. Hooper came here to see you. She ordered you to behave yourself or . . . ?"

Mr. Wetherhead bowed his head. "Or she'd turn Miranda in to the drug squad."

Nicholas's eyes met mine across the kitchen table. He looked as bewildered as I felt.

"Pardon?" he said. "Did I hear you correctly? Did you say the, er, *drug* squad?"

"It's all lies!" Mr. Wetherhead's head came up, and his face was desperate. "Miranda's herbal remedies are as wholesome as my granny's chamomile tea. There's no question of her using illegal substances. Miranda may be a witch, but she's a law-abiding witch. I'll swear to it."

"Is that what you told Mrs. Hooper?" Nicholas asked.

Mr. Wetherhead glowered. "What I said to Pruneface Hooper isn't fit to repeat in mixed company."

Nicholas's face remained impassive. "Did you tell Ms. Morrow of Mrs. Hooper's unfounded accusation?"

"I had to, didn't I?" The little man was pleading now. "Miranda had to know what she was up against. When I told her, she laughed and said that the Prunefaces of the world had been holding matches to her feet for hundreds of years but they hadn't burnt her yet because . . . because *witches know how to protect themselves*." He paused to take a shuddering breath.

"That's why you suspect Ms. Morrow of killing Mrs. Hooper," Nicholas clarified. "You thought Finch's resident witch might have been protecting herself." He leaned back in his chair and gazed at Mr. Wetherhead reflectively. "Why would Ms. Morrow need to protect herself if Mrs. Hooper wasn't telling the truth about the herbal remedies?"

"I could be wrong," Mr. Wetherhead said doggedly. "There's others who could've done it. Billy Barlow could've. Mrs. Taxman was saying only this morning that Billy was on the square early that day, and he hated old Pruneface's guts."

"Why did he dislike her so intensely?" Nicholas inquired.

"She kicked his terrier," Mr. Wetherhead replied. "I saw her do it, right there in front of the Emporium, the Sunday before she died."

I gasped. "Pruneface kicked *Buster?*"

Mr. Wetherhead nodded eagerly. "Claimed Buster'd nipped her grandson. More likely the other way round, if you ask me, but Pruneface lashed out at Buster anyway. I thought Billy Barlow would throttle her on the spot." Mr. Wetherhead's face brightened suddenly, as though a ray of hope had shone through the dark cloud of his foreboding. "He's disappeared, hasn't he? No one knows where he's gone or when he's coming back. He's on the run, is my guess." He pointed at Nicholas. "You concentrate on finding Billy Barlow and leave Miranda out of it."

"It may not be possible to leave Ms.

Morrow out of it," Nicholas told him, "but I'm grateful to you for speaking with us." He stood. "Would you be willing to listen to a word of advice from a younger, less experienced man?"

The dark cloud had settled once more over Mr. Wetherhead, but he nodded.

"All of this sneaking about is doing more harm than good to Ms. Morrow's reputation," said Nicholas. "I suggest you reschedule your treatments during normal business hours."

Mr. Wetherhead put his head in his hands and groaned. "You don't understand," he said. "There won't be any more treatments if your so-called search for truth lands Miranda in prison."

It was still raining. Nicholas and I stood beneath the peaked roof sheltering Mr. Wetherhead's front door and contemplated the dense thorn hedge that shielded Briar Cottage from Saint George's Lane.

"Our next stop," said Nicholas. "I'm rather looking forward to meeting Ms. Morrow."

"She won't be bullied as easily as Mr. Wetherhead," I muttered.

Nicholas took a deep breath. "I wondered when you'd get around to scolding me." He scuffed his shoe against the doorstep. "I thought you knew what to expect, Lori. You're the one who said we'd need dynamite to open Mr. Wetherhead's mouth."

"I know." I hunched my shoulders as a gust of wind splashed rain against my face. "I just didn't expect you to be so . . . explosive."

"We're dealing with murder," Nicholas reminded me. "We can't always afford to be polite."

"I'd advise you to be polite with Miranda Morrow," I warned, glancing up at him, "or she'll turn both of us into frogs."

"You'd make a fetching frog." He smiled crookedly. "Am I forgiven?"

"There's nothing to forgive," I admitted. "You got the information we wanted. I suppose I can't carp too much about your methods."

"Frogs and carp." Nicholas dabbed a raindrop from the tip of my nose. "You've been in the wet too long, Lori. It's coloring your vocabulary."

I laughed, but as Nicholas turned up the collar of his trench coat and peered at the leaden sky, I couldn't keep myself from worrying about his methods. I didn't mind questioning my neighbors or surveilling them from a distance, but I wasn't willing to shout at them or sneak up to their windows or threaten to sic the cops on them if they refused to speak with us.

Nicholas seemed willing to do anything. What had started as a casual pursuit had at some point become for him something far more serious. Why was he pushing so hard? Was he driven by a sense of duty to his aunt and uncle, or by a compulsion I did not yet understand? As we approached Briar Cottage I couldn't help wondering just how far he'd go to find out who'd killed Pruneface Hooper.

Chapter
15

Briar Cottage's front garden was a haven for plants most people despised. Once through the squeaky gate in Miranda's thorn hedge, Nicholas and I found ourselves surrounded by beds of nettles, thistles, and teasels, which would, in a few short weeks, be joined by dock, ragwort, speedwell, spurge, and the perennial summer favorite, dandelions. The pesky intruders that drove most gardeners insane were welcome here: Miranda tended her weeds as lovingly as Emma Harris tended her roses.

"The source of Ms. Morrow's herbal remedies, I assume," said Nicholas, surveying the curious collection.

"She grows hemlock and deadly nightshade in a greenhouse out back," I informed him. "Lucky for her Mrs. Hooper wasn't poisoned."

"Indeed." Nicholas looked at the cottage. "It's a pretty place."

I agreed with him. I loved everything about

Briar Cottage, from its shaggy thatched roof to its lichen-mottled stone walls. It was a shade too small to accommodate a growing family, but for a single woman living with a cat, it was ideal.

Miranda Morrow opened the front door before we had a chance to ring the bell. A true believer might have surmised precognition, but I suspected a more mundane explanation, which Miranda soon confirmed.

"Lori!" she exclaimed. "How delicious to see you. George rang to warn me of your visit."

Miranda's eyes, like Nicholas's, were green, but whereas his were flecked with blue and gold, hers were as pure as emeralds. She was in her mid-thirties, and her wholesome good looks defied clichéd descriptions of ugly witches. Her nose was sprinkled with freckles instead of warts, and her waist-length hair was strawberry-blond, not grizzled gray. She wore a long pale green sweater over an ankle-length skirt made of a swirling patchwork of yellow and gold velvet.

Miranda's green eyes narrowed as they fell on Nicholas's face. She studied him in silence for perhaps thirty seconds before saying, "I know who *you* are, darling."

"I'm Nicholas Fox," he said. "Lilian Bunting's nephew."

"So I've been told." She stepped aside. "Come in, you splendid creatures, and warm yourselves before my fire."

Miranda's front room was cluttered with the tools of her trade. Tarot cards, faceted crystals, dousing twigs, and a miscellany of arcane paraphernalia littered the rough wood-beam mantelpiece, astral charts covered the walls, and bunches of dried herbs hung from the smoke-darkened rafters, filling the room with a pleasantly pungent mélange of fragrances.

Miranda may have used the cards, crystals, and charts as reference tools, but she depended on modern technology to earn a living. She was a telephone witch, dispensing advice, readings, and predictions to all who called. Her state-of-the-art computerized switchboard was tucked discreetly in a nook beneath the stairs to keep it from spoiling the cottage's distinctly pretechnological ambience.

Miranda hung our coats on pegs protruding from the door and motioned for us to be seated on a fat little sofa draped with paisley shawls and set at an angle to the red-brick hearth.

"I'd like to thank you," she said to Nicholas as she bent to add coals to the fire. "I can't tell you how grateful I am to you for convincing George to dispense with secrecy."

"I wasn't aware that I had convinced him," said Nicholas.

"He told me you were most persuasive." Silver rings glinted on Miranda's fingers as she caressed a black cat curled on the burgundy-fringed ottoman. The cat opened its luminous yellow eyes, bumped its head against Miranda's knuckles, tucked its nose under its paws, and went back to sleep. "Seraphina isn't alarmed by you," Miranda noted. "Should I be?"

Nicholas smiled. "Ms. Morrow —"

"Miranda, darling. We don't stand on ceremony here. Not the usual ceremony, at any rate." She sat in an overstuffed armchair that was set, like the sofa, at a slight angle to the hearth. "I shall call you . . . Nicholas. He's the patron saint of wolves, I believe. Have you come to Finch seeking prey?"

"I've come seeking the truth," said Nicholas. "I want to find out who murdered Prunella Hooper."

"So, presumably, do the police," Miranda murmured.

"My aunt tells me that the villagers aren't cooperating with the police," Nicholas said. "No one's come forward with information."

"That's where you come in, is it?" There

was a taunting lilt to Miranda's voice. "Scrounging for tidbits to feed to the authorities?"

"I'm doing what needs to be done to give my aunt and uncle peace of mind," Nicholas answered calmly.

I spoke up. "We're trying to help Kit Smith, too. The police are treating him as a suspect."

"Sweet Kit? A suspect in a murder inquiry?" Miranda rolled her eyes heavenward. "I thought we'd already scaled the heights of absurdity, but I can see we've a ways to go yet. What utter rot."

"I'm with you," I assured her. "But the police aren't, and the pressure's getting to Kit. If this case doesn't break soon, I'm afraid he will."

"Poor lamb," Miranda cooed. "First Mrs. Hooper picks on him and now the police."

My ears pricked up. "You've heard the nasty story Mrs. Hooper concocted?"

"Had it straight from the source." Miranda folded her legs beneath her and shook her hair back from her face. "She came here one day not long before she died. Brought me a potted geranium. She said she was being neighborly, but I knew what her game was the moment I laid eyes on her."

"Did you invite her in?" Nicholas asked.

"Naturally. I knew I'd have to purify the place after she left, but her brand of pathology fascinates me." Miranda stretched her arm out dramatically. "Evil incarnate, offering me a potted plant. I leapt at the chance to observe her at close quarters." Miranda's gaze fell on me. "She sat where you're sitting now."

Her gaze lingered long enough to make me acutely aware of how small the fat little sofa was. Nicholas couldn't help pressing his thigh against mine. There was nowhere else for it to go.

Miranda seemed to sense that it wasn't the fire's warmth alone that brought a flush to my cheeks. Her eyes twinkled merrily as she went on.

"We had a scrumptious chin-wag," she said. "She'd been collecting tidbits, too, pinpricks of poison sprinkled judiciously into the chatter. Had I heard that Sally Pyne hated little boys? Did I know that Dick Peacock was engaged in shady dealings? What about Mr. Barlow's vicious terrier? Wouldn't I agree that Buster should, for safety's sake, be put down?"

"Good grief," I muttered.

"The nonsense was presented so artfully, with so much charm, that I wanted to applaud." Miranda's green eyes flashed. "Until she came to Kit. When she told me he'd taken advantage of Nell Harris, I simply had to laugh."

"You laughed?" I said, nonplussed.

"What else could I do?" Miranda shrugged. "It was the best joke I'd heard in years. Sweet Kit assaulting Nell the Invincible? I think not."

"Did you voice your opinion?" inquired Nicholas.

"I told Mrs. Hooper that I envied her," Miranda replied. "Most gardeners are forced to labor over heaps of compost, but she could manure her geraniums simply by talking to them."

I snickered, Nicholas grinned, and Miranda sighed with pleasure, as if reliving the memorable moment.

"I imagine she was offended," Nicholas said dryly.

"It took a moment for the insult to register, but once it did, yes, she was offended." Miranda studied the silver rings on her left hand. "That's when she began lecturing me on my morals."

"Had she seen you visiting George Wetherhead?" I asked.

"Watching us was, apparently, her idea of early-morning entertainment," said Miranda. "She had our schedule by heart. She accused me of corrupting an innocent."

"She accused George of philandering," I told her.

"Lovely!" Miranda clapped her hands. "Men like George so rarely get the chance to be seen as naughty boys."

"He was pretty upset by it," I said.

"Was he?" A puzzled frown crossed Miranda's face. She tilted her head back, as if giving the matter profound consideration, and murmured, "I wonder if *I* should be offended?"

Nicholas, too, looked upward, at the bundled herbs hanging from the rafters. His glance seemed perfunctory, but I felt his body tense as his gaze came to rest on a gap between two of the bundles.

He looked at Miranda. "How did you respond to Mrs. Hooper's accusation?"

Miranda shook her head mournfully. "I told her that jealousy was a sad emotion and that I'd be perfectly willing to step aside if she wanted George for herself."

"You *didn't*," I said, delighted.

"I *did*." Miranda ran a finger along her skirt's patchwork seams. "That's when she began to discuss the unusual variety of plants in my garden. She was under the impression that I'd not only corrupted George's morals but introduced him to the demon weed as well."

"Marijuana?" I said. "What made her think you grow pot?"

"My herbs, presumably." Miranda swept a hand through the air to indicate the bundles overhead. "I cultivate medicinal plants, but to a woman with Mrs. Hooper's vicious imagination, any medicine that isn't dispensed by a chemist is automatically suspect."

"Marijuana has therapeutic applications," Nicholas pointed out.

"True." Miranda went on speaking as she got up to toss more coal onto the fire. "Its use in treating glaucoma is well documented. It can also help to reduce nausea and increase appetite in people undergoing chemotherapy or radiation treatment. It can work the same way for people afflicted with AIDS. It's an extremely useful plant."

"It must be frustrating to be unable to use it," Nicholas commented.

"It is," Miranda agreed. She dusted the palms of her hands together lightly and returned to her chair. "But its production must be specially licensed."

"Do you have such a license, Miranda?" Nicholas asked.

"I do not," she answered. "Which is why you'll find no marijuana on these premises."

Nicholas said nothing. He merely turned

his gaze to the gap in the hanging bundles of dried herbs.

"It is my belief, however," Miranda continued, "that folk medicine belongs to the people, not to a medical board. I said as much to Mrs. Hooper when she threatened to bring the drug squad down on me."

Nicholas raised an eyebrow. "She threatened you, did she?"

"I'd insulted her twice in the course of one conversation, darling. She couldn't allow me to get away scot-free, could she, Seraphina?" Miranda scooped the black cat up from the ottoman. "She lost her temper — and her charm — and tried to frighten us. We told her to bring the drug squad to tea, didn't we, my sweet?" Miranda cradled Seraphina on her shoulder.

"I wonder . . ." Nicholas rubbed his jaw. "Do you think she threatened anyone else in Finch?"

"Everyone, I should imagine," said Miranda. "She couldn't help herself. Her spirit was distorted, twisted, ravaged by fear. Fear makes some people timid — look at what it's done to poor George — but it turns others into devouring monsters."

"What was she afraid of?" I asked.

"Everything, anything . . ." Miranda fluttered her fingers nonchalantly. "She needed to be in control of every situation, darling, and she used any means at her disposal to gain the upper hand."

"Lies, threats, intimidation," Nicholas murmured.

"That's not all." Miranda's green eyes drifted lazily toward Nicholas. "Just ask Peggy Taxman."

Nicholas stiffened, but his voice betrayed only a faint perplexity.

"I understood that Mrs. Taxman and Mrs. Hooper were old friends," he said. "Aunt Lilian told me that they knew each other when they lived in Birmingham."

"Peggy's distraught over Mrs. Hooper's death," I added. "She visits the grave every day. Lilian told us that she must be spending a small fortune on flowers."

Miranda tossed her head dismissively. "Guilt gelt and crocodile tears. If you ask me, she visits the grave in order to reassure herself that Mrs. Hooper is still dead."

"You must know something we don't know," Nicholas said. "Care to share it?"

Instead of answering directly, Miranda asked a question in return. "Did you know that Peggy allowed Mrs. Hooper to live in Crabtree Cottage gratis?" She rolled the *r* in *gratis* to give it extra emphasis.

"Peggy wasn't collecting rent?" I asked.

"I knew it would surprise you," said Miranda.

I turned to Nicholas. "I've never known Peggy Taxman to give anything away for free."

"She did this time." Miranda nuzzled Seraphina's ears. "I overheard Peggy and her husband going at it one day in the Emporium's back room. Jasper was indignant. He wanted to know why Mrs. Hooper was living in the cottage free of charge. Not only that . . ." Miranda smiled lazily. "It seems the accounts weren't balancing properly. Certain sums of money had gone missing, and Jasper wanted to know what Peggy had done with them. The spat suggested a certain something to me. Can you guess what it is?"

I was stumped, but Nicholas wasn't.

"Blackmail," he said promptly.

"You'd make a yummy constable." Miranda puckered her lips in his direction. "So quick off the mark with deductions. But I'm afraid they'd make you trim your lovely hair, which in itself would be a crime."

"I assume you reached the same conclusion," Nicholas said patiently.

"Mrs. Hooper was a charter member of Backstabbers Anonymous," Miranda declared. "The only thing she used friends for was target practice."

"Mrs. Hooper was blackmailing Peggy?" I said, scrambling to catch up.

"Well done, Lori. Slow but steady wins the race." Miranda spoke lightly, but her eyes were deadly serious. "I believe that Mrs. Hooper threatened to reveal something Peggy didn't want broadcast, some naughtiness from the good old days in Birmingham, perhaps. Peggy thought Crabtree Cottage would buy her old chum's silence, but I'll wager that Mrs. Hooper wanted more."

"Hence the missing sums of money," said Nicholas.

"Malevolent creatures like Mrs. Hooper always want more." Miranda returned Seraphina to the ottoman. "Ignorant people call them witches. I can think of a more appropriate term."

"Thank you, Miranda." Nicholas got to his feet and put a hand out to help me to mine. "I've enjoyed our conversation."

"I spoke to you for Kit's sake," Miranda stated flatly. "I've glimpsed his spirit, too, and it's pure as the driven snow. I won't have him harassed."

"I'm grateful nonetheless," said Nicholas. "I hope we'll meet again."

"You can bring the drug squad with you to tea." Miranda's green eyes twinkled as she walked us to the door. They twinkled more happily still when Nicholas held my jacket for me while I slipped into it.

"It's a pity Mrs. Hooper died when she did," she commented. "She would have had a field day with the two of you." She paused. "But in your case, my pets, I wonder . . . Would she have been lying?"

"Miranda," I began, but Nicholas interrupted.

"She's teasing us, Lori," he said. "Aren't you, Miranda?"

"I read auras, darling," she replied. "And yours is . . . most revealing."

When we reached the thorn hedge, Nicholas paused for another look at Briar Cottage.

"You're convinced that Miranda had marijuana hanging from the rafters." I tried to sound businesslike, as if Nicholas's aura was of no concern to me. "You think she got rid of it after Mrs. Hooper issued her threats."

"It's a distinct possibility," Nicholas allowed. "As Mr. Wetherhead pointed out, witches know how to protect themselves. Our witch seems to have protected herself by employing the simple expedient of covering her tracks."

"Can we scratch her from our list of murder suspects?" I asked.

"Definitely." Nicholas opened the squeaky gate. "If Miranda Morrow had killed Mrs. Hooper, the coroner's verdict would have been natural causes."

Chapter
16

Nicholas and I agreed to put off speaking with Peggy Taxman until the next day. My energy was beginning to flag and I still had a three-mile bike ride ahead of me. By the time I reached the cottage, I knew I'd be in desperate need of a hot bath, a hearty lunch, and a long nap.

Nicholas, too, was in need of a break. We'd accumulated a lot of information in a short amount of time. He wanted to spend the rest of the day cogitating and, I suspected, enjoying a pleasant doze in the vicar's study.

I left him at the vicarage and went to collect my things from Wysteria Lodge. I let myself in through the front door this time. It didn't matter much if people saw me. My cover was already blown.

The moment I entered the office, I made a beeline for the desk, picked up the telephone, and punched in Bill's London number. I wanted to tell him about the stakeout and the morning's interviews, but most of all, I wanted to hear his voice. My head, and probably my aura, were too full of Nicholas. I needed to reclaim space for my husband.

The conversation didn't go quite as smoothly as I'd planned.

Bill was relieved to hear that I'd survived the stakeout unscathed and let me ramble on at length about George Wetherhead, Miranda Morrow, and Peggy Taxman. In the course of my rambling, however, I somehow strayed onto a path I'd intended to avoid.

"Bill," I said, swiveling in his desk chair to face the window, "when you get back, you're going to hear a lot of talk about me and Nicholas. It's nonsense, of course, but —"

"Is it?" There was a pause. "You're not possessed by a demonic spirit again, are you?"

"Huh?"

"If I remember correctly, that's what happened to you up in Northumberland last fall, when you —"

"Bill —"

"— fell into the arms of . . . What was his name? Well-built guy, curly black hair . . . Adam! That's it. Adam Chase. I know you couldn't help yourself with Adam, but I'd hoped you'd exercise a modicum of self-restraint with Nicholas. Unless, of course, you're possessed by a demonic spirit, in which case all is forgiven."

I gave him a chance to catch his breath. His caustic comments stung, but I was in no position to object to them. My husband had every right to take me to task.

"I'm not possessed," I said evenly. "And I've been exercising a great deal of self-restraint."

"Have you needed to?" Bill asked.

"Yes." I groaned and leaned my head on my hand. "I'm sorry, but it's true. Come on, Bill. Haven't you ever been attracted to someone other than me?"

"As a matter of fact, I have."

My head came up. "Really?"

"Not as often as you, perhaps," he replied testily, "but there have been moments."

"Oh." I blinked stupidly at the telephone. I wasn't sure how I felt. One part of me was stunned by his admission, but a larger part was relieved. I rested my elbows on the desk and asked, "Why do you suppose that is?"

"I don't know." The sarcasm had left his voice. He sounded a bit sad, but mostly thoughtful, as if he truly were trying to figure out why two people who loved each other as much as we did would ever consider turning to anyone else. "It has nothing to do with love. I've never loved anyone but you."

"It happens to me when I'm running around with someone, chasing after something." I looked out of the window at the pub and remembered the way my heart had raced when I'd seen Nicholas in the storeroom. "Maybe it's nothing to do with Nicholas. Maybe it's the excitement, the thrill of the chase, spilling over onto him."

"If that's the case, there's a simple solution," Bill said. "You and I have to have some adventures of our own."

I sat up, enchanted by the idea. "Yeah? You have anything in mind?"

A warm tingle passed through me when I heard the smile in Bill's voice.

"I can't guarantee another murder," he said, "but I'll think of something."

"I'll work on it, too," I promised. "In the meantime, please don't let the gossip worry you. I haven't done anything with Nicholas that I couldn't do in front of our sons."

"Not a bad guide to behavior," Bill said dryly. "Perhaps we should both bear it in mind." He took a deep breath and let it out slowly. "I'm glad we've . . . talked."

"So am I," I said. "We can talk more when you get home, if you like."

"Talk isn't what I had in mind," said Bill, "but we can certainly add it to the agenda. Good luck with Peggy Taxman, love."

"Thanks," I said. "I'll need it. See you on Saturday."

I hung up the phone and sat for a long time, gazing at Reginald. He looked back at me with an oddly satisfied gleam in his black button eyes.

"Well, what do you know?" I said finally. "My saintly husband is human, after all. He can lose his temper, run out of patience, and admit to feeling some old-fashioned extra-marital lust." I poked Reginald in his pink-flannel tummy and laughed out loud. "Call me crazy, Reg, but I don't think I've ever loved Bill more than I do right this minute."

The unanticipated detour in my conversation with Bill reenergized me, so the bike ride home wasn't the ordeal I'd been dreading. The rain let up, the wind abated, and I pedaled slowly, relishing the beauty of the blossoming trees I passed along the way. Apple, pear, and cherry had sprung into bloom overnight, brightening the dreary day with a fluttering snowstorm of white and pink petals.

Will and Rob were as happy to see me as I was to see them, and I quickly absolved Annelise of all responsibility for making lunch. After yet another change of clothes, I prepared a batch of mushroom crepes and an enormous spinach-and-bacon salad, and filled the leftover crepes with raspberry jam for dessert. The twins requested scrambled-egg sandwiches — their latest food fad — but they made a dent in the jam crepes as well.

Once they were down for their naps, I indulged in a steamy bath, then stretched out on the bed for an hour. I awakened feeling refreshed and ready to spend the remainder of the afternoon keeping up with my bouncing boys. It wasn't until they were in bed and asleep after dinner that I had a chance to shut myself in the study and make my report to Aunt Dimity.

"The long and the short of it is that nearly everyone with whom we've spoken had a reason to want Prunella Hooper dead," I concluded.

I curled up in the tall leather armchair and waited for Dimity's response. I'd turned the lamps off when I'd lit the fire and so watched her words unfurl by the light of the leaping flames.

Mrs. Hooper wounded Sally Pyne's pride, kicked Billy Barlow's dog, spread scurrilous lies about Kit, witnessed Dick Peacock's suspicious behavior, terrorized George Wetherhead, and threatened Miranda Morrow. She may also have been blackmailing Peggy Taxman.

"She kept busy," I acknowledged. "Any of them could have done it, Dimity. Most were out and about at the right time, and it wouldn't have required exceptional strength to crack Mrs. Hooper's skull."

Let's review their activities, shall we? On the morning in question, Mr. Barlow was walking his killer terrier on the square; Mr. Peacock was in front of his pub, possibly receiving smuggled goods; and Miss Morrow was returning from a mission of mercy to Mr. Wetherhead. We will assume for the moment that Kit was where he said he was, tending the horses at Anscombe Manor. Where was Sally Pyne?

I shrugged. "Watching Dick Peacock from the tearoom, I suppose. She seems to know what he does every Thursday morning."

And Peggy Taxman?

"In bed, I think." I recalled the conversation Nicholas and I had had with Peggy over Pruneface Hooper's grave. "She told us that she'd heard Mr. Barlow was up early, but she didn't say she'd seen him."

There stands Crabtree Cottage, in the midst of an inordinate amount of bustle, yet no one notices anyone enter the cottage, confront Mrs. Hooper, and smack her in the head. It's most annoying.

"Maybe Peggy Taxman holds the key," I said. "And there's Mr. Barlow to consider, if he ever comes back from wherever he is. But I agree with Nicholas about Miranda Morrow. If Miranda had killed Pruneface, she would have used something more subtle than a blunt instrument."

How are you getting on with Nicholas?

"We've had our ups and downs." I stretched my legs out on the leather ottoman and looked toward the ivy-webbed window over the desk. "I wonder if he watches cop shows."

Excuse me?

"Police programs," I explained, "on television."

What a curious thing to wonder.

"There's an interrogation technique they use on cop shows," I explained. "It's called the good cop/bad cop routine. One officer's nice, his partner's mean, and between them they get the suspect to spill the beans."

Go on.

"The thing is, Nicholas was playing both roles when we spoke with George Wetherhead — good and bad — and he was incredibly good at it, turned it on and off just like that." I snapped my fingers. "I didn't like it. It scared me."

Why did it scare you?

"I guess . . ." I ran a hand through my dark curls. "I guess it makes me wonder which one is the real Nicholas — the good cop or the bad cop."

Ask your sons.

I smiled at the suggestion. "They'd be biased. He bribed them with toys."

Do Rob and Will always accept the bribes offered them?

Dimity's question brought to mind an incident that had taken place during our visit to Boston. I stared at the darkened window and recalled a particular afternoon in early February when Bill's aunts had insisted on introducing their grandnephews to a politician friend.

The man had seemed okay to me and Bill, but the boys had refused to accept the toy boats he'd brought along especially for them. They had, in fact, refused to go anywhere near the guy and stood clinging to my father-in-law's immaculately creased trouser legs throughout the visit. We found out later that the politician had been instrumental in cutting public funding for day care.

"No," I said. "No, they don't." I slid my hand along the arm of the chair and added sheepishly, "It sounds silly, Dimity, but they seem to be pretty good judges of character."

It doesn't sound silly to me. Why shouldn't your sons be good judges of character? Some children are blessed with a special ability to see through masks and playacting to the heart of a person's truest self. They may not have the words to express their opinions, but they have other ways of making them known.

Will and Rob had taken a genuine liking to Nicholas, right off the bat. They'd romped with him, rifled his pockets, and clambered in and out of his lap during lunch. As far as my sons were concerned, Nicholas was good cop through and through.

"Thanks, Dimity," I said. "I like Nicholas, and I didn't want to think badly of him. You — and the boys — have helped me to see him more clearly."

I don't wish to muddy the waters, my dear, but Nicholas's behavior does seem a tiny bit odd to me.

"In what way?" I asked.

He seems to be fond of you — in a purely collegial sense, of course. He also depends on you to smooth the way for him with the villagers. Am I correct?

It seemed politic to skip over Nicholas's noncollegial feelings for me, so I answered with a simple "Yes."

Why, then, was he willing to display a persona so disagreeable that it threatened to alienate you from him? It strikes me as a risky and extreme measure. Why is Nicholas willing to go to such lengths to discover who killed a woman with whom he had no personal connection?

"He's concerned about his aunt and uncle," I offered.

What a very good nephew he is. Strange that he doesn't visit his aunt and uncle more often. Were the Buntings by any chance among the teeming masses thronging the square on the fateful morning?

"No, Dimity," I said, grinning. "Lilian and the vicar seem to be the only people in Finch who weren't up at dawn."

Thank God for small favors. My dear Lori, your day has been full of sound and fury, but there's no telling yet what it signifies. I shall be most interested to hear the results of your interview with Mrs. Taxman. Sleep well. You'll need your wits about you if you're bearding the lioness in her den tomorrow.

"Good night, Dimity." I closed the journal and sat quietly with it resting on my lap.

It had been a long day, filled with unexpected twists and turns. I felt as if I'd opened a window on my neighbors' secret lives. Each had something to hide, some reason to be ashamed, angry, or fearful, and each thought someone else had a better reason than his or her own to kill Mrs. Hooper. Finch had once appeared to me to be a quiet backwater. I knew now that it was roiling with turbulent undercurrents.

I slid the journal into its niche on the bookshelves, twiddled Reginald's ears, and stood for a moment, gazing into the fire. I felt as if I'd opened a window on my marriage as well. Bill and I had never spoken openly about my wandering eye, nor had he ever before admitted to having one of his own. I welcomed the revelation and hoped it would stir us both to action. Our relationship had become too settled, too predictable. It needed a good shaking to keep it from sinking under the weight of its own stability.

I hated to admit it, but I owed a debt of gratitude to the late and unlamented Pruneface Hooper. Her vile behavior and violent death had shed new light on my neighbors' lives and, indirectly, on my own.

Chapter
17

Kitchen's Emporium stood opposite Sally Pyne's tearoom on the square. Its white-framed display window featured a tidy pyramid of baked-bean cans flanked by a shiny lawn mower and a bolt of chintz fabric. The unusual juxtaposition of items signaled to all comers that Kitchen's Emporium was the most general of general stores. I'd long since ceased to be amazed by the variety of items Peggy Taxman stashed in her voluminous storeroom. Whether I needed a set of wrenches or a sack of flour, I could rest assured that the Emporium would provide.

The sun was peeking furtively from behind a wash of gray clouds when I bumped over the humpbacked bridge the following morning. It was Friday. I had one more day to spend with Nicholas before my husband returned home. I was looking forward to it.

Nicholas and I had agreed to meet at the Emporium at ten o'clock, but as I pulled into the square, I spotted him standing by the war memorial. He was dressed in his tweed blazer, creamy turtleneck, and dark brown trousers, but he carried his trench coat over his arm, as insurance. I parked the Rover in front of the Emporium, grabbed my jacket from the backseat, and walked over to join him.

"Sleep well?" he inquired when I'd stepped through the holly hedge.

"Very," I replied. "You?"

"Not as well as I'd hoped." He rocked back on his heels and peered up at the worn Celtic cross. "I had a lecture from my aunt last night."

"Ah." I, too, turned my attention to the cross. "About us?"

"Yes." He glanced at me briefly, then clasped his hands behind his back and looked up again. "I explained to her that nothing untoward had happened between us, and she explained to me that anyone with a functioning brain could tell that something *would* happen if we didn't exercise extreme caution."

I gave the square's façades a surly stare. "Does everyone in this town read auras?" I demanded petulantly. "Or are they all supremely gifted with that sixth sense you were telling me about?"

Nicholas's smile was delightful but short-lived. He bowed his head and said somberly, "They read glances, Lori. They read gestures and tones of voice, and they're not far wrong, are they?"

"No," I admitted with a sigh. "They're pretty much right on the money."

Concern clouded Nicholas's bright eyes. "I don't want our association to cause trouble for you after I've gone."

"There won't be any trouble I can't handle," I assured him.

"And your husband?" Nicholas asked. "Will he be able to handle it?"

"Bill and I will be fine," I said. "We'll be better than fine, in fact. You can tell your aunt that you've been instrumental in bringing us closer together."

"Have I?" He looked pleased but puzzled.

"Let's just say that you've helped us open a new line of communication," I told him, "one we've needed to open for quite some time."

"Glad to be of service," he said.

"As for everyone else . . ." A demon must have whispered in my ear at that moment because I couldn't keep myself from leaning forward and smooching Nicholas full on the lips. "There," I said, stepping back in triumph. "Now we've *really* given them something to talk about."

Nicholas gaped at me, nonplussed, then threw back his head and laughed. "You're a wicked woman, Lori Shepherd."

"I'm performing a public service," I declared airily. "They've been too wrapped up in themselves and Mrs. Hooper for too long. Let 'em sink their teeth into me for a change. I can take it — and so can Bill."

"I sincerely hope so, for your sake." Nicholas touched his mouth, then shook a finger at me. "But you must never, ever, do that again. As I told you, I'm not —"

"— beyond temptation. I know." I cocked my head to one side and regarded him thoughtfully. "But I think I may be." I tucked my hand into the crook of his arm. "Come on, old bean. We've got a lioness to beard."

The jangle of sleigh bells announced our arrival at the Emporium. Nicholas closed the bell-adorned door behind us as I paused to survey the shop. A computerized cash register had replaced the Emporium's ancient model, but nothing else had changed since I'd last been there.

To our right stood a long wooden counter with a grilled window at the far end, denoting the post office. The space to our left was filled with shelves and racks holding a colorful array of groceries, toiletries, and assorted odds and ends. A small brown door at the rear of the shop led to Peggy's wondrous storeroom.

Jasper Taxman perched on a wooden stool behind the counter. He and Peggy could still be considered newlyweds, since they'd been married for less than a year, but he looked as if he'd always been behind the counter of Peggy's shop.

He was extraordinarily nondescript — his brown suit and tie matched his brown hair and eyes — but a passionate heart beat beneath his bland exterior. He'd astonished the village once, by breaking the law to keep Peggy from leaving Finch. I had little doubt that he'd do it again, to keep her from going to prison.

He stood as Nicholas and I approached the counter.

"Good morning, Mr. Taxman," I said. "I don't believe you've met Lilian Bunting's nephew. May I introduce Nicholas Fox?"

I wasn't surprised that Jasper had allowed me to make the introduction without interruption. Peggy's husband was as reticent as he was nondescript. I pitied the poor policeman who'd tried to question him.

"How do you do?" he said, nodding to Nicholas.

"Very well indeed, sir," said Nicholas. "And you?"

Mr. Taxman stepped forward to face Nicholas across the counter. "I am extremely worried about my wife."

Now I was surprised. Mr. Taxman rarely offered information of any kind to anyone. For him to comment on such a personal subject to a complete stranger was, to my knowledge, unprecedented.

"Sally Pyne tells me that you're making an informal inquiry into the death of Prunella Hooper," Mr. Taxman went on. "I would urge you to speak with my wife."

"Why?" asked Nicholas.

Mr. Taxman gazed down at the counter in silence. When he looked up again, his brow was furrowed, and his eyes were dark with apprehension. "Peggy isn't behaving . . . normally, Mr. Fox. She hasn't behaved normally since Mrs. Hooper came to Finch, and now that Mrs. Hooper is dead, her behavior continues to be . . . abnormal."

Nicholas laid his trench coat across the counter. "Can you tell us what you mean by abnormal?"

Mr. Taxman glanced toward the front entrance, as if to reassure himself that we wouldn't be disturbed. When he saw no customers peering through the display window, he gave Nicholas his full attention once again.

"My wife has run the Emporium success-fully for eleven years," he began. "It's not been easy for her. Competitors in sur-rounding towns spring up every day, tempting her regulars to shop elsewhere."

Nicholas looked over his shoulder at the bulging shelves. "Her business appears to be doing well."

"It's doing well," said Mr. Taxman, "be-cause Peggy keeps a tight hold on the purse strings. I was a professional accountant be-fore my retirement, but there's nothing I could teach my wife about money manage-ment."

"Does your wife's abnormal behavior have something to do with money?" Nich-olas prompted.

"It has everything to do with money." Mr. Taxman rubbed his furrowed brow. "Peggy allowed Prunella Hooper to live in Crabtree Cottage free of charge. She removed sums of money from the till without accounting for them properly. She's throwing money away on flowers to put on Prunella Hooper's grave. It's not like her to be so frivolous, sir, not like her at all."

Nicholas inclined his head toward Mr. Taxman. "Did you mention any of this to the police?"

Jasper lowered his eyes. "It was none of their business. My wife had nothing to do with Mrs. Hooper's death."

"Was your wife with you that morning?" Nicholas asked.

"She was in the storeroom, taking inventory." Mr. Taxman gestured toward the brown door. "She'd been up all night."

It was an evasive reply, but Nicholas didn't push. Instead, he addressed what was, to me, a more interesting subject.

"What do you know of Mrs. Hooper?"

Mr. Taxman shrugged. "She and Peggy grew up together in Birmingham. They lived on the same street, went to the same schools, worked at the same shop. They lost track of each other after Peggy married Mr. Kitchen, her first husband, but when Mrs. Hooper's husband died last year, she contacted Peggy."

"I see." Nicholas pursed his lips. "Did your wife invite Mrs. Hooper to live in Crabtree Cottage?"

Mr. Taxman lifted his palms toward the ceiling. "I don't know whose idea it was for Mrs. Hooper to come to Finch," he said, "but I wish to God she'd stayed away."

"Mr. Taxman, I don't mean to offend you," said Nicholas, "but your wife's pattern of behavior suggests that she may have been subjected to some form of blackmail by Mrs. Hooper. Has such a possibility presented itself to you?"

"It has," admitted Mr. Taxman. "But I have no idea what kind of hold Mrs. Hooper might have had over my wife. Peggy is a formidable woman, but she's led a blameless life. She has strict moral standards and a keen sense of social responsibility. She's been a pillar of every community she's called home." He looked at me. "Ask Lori if you don't believe me. Peggy's dedicated her life to Finch, hasn't she, Lori?"

I could have said a word or two about Peggy's strict moral standards — Kit had felt their sharp end, as had Nicholas and I — but decided to comment only on her community spirit.

"We depend on Peggy," I told Nicholas. "She organizes nearly every activity in the village."

Nicholas gazed at Mr. Taxman reflectively. "Have you broached the subject of blackmail with your wife?"

"I've tried." Mr. Taxman seemed to wilt. "Peggy won't talk to me. She won't tell me what's troubling her." He looked imploringly at Nicholas. "Please, Mr. Fox, make her talk to you. Sally Pyne said you could charm water from a rock. Please make my wife tell you what she won't tell me."

Nicholas studied Mr. Taxman's face before saying, "It may be something you don't want to hear."

"I don't care!" Mr. Taxman cried. He laid his palms flat on the counter as if to steady himself. "I will stand by my wife no matter what, but until I know what's wrong, I can do nothing to help her. Please, sir, help me to help my wife."

Nicholas looked at the brown door at the rear of the shop. "Is she here?"

Mr. Taxman shook his head. "She's at the churchyard, visiting that vile woman's grave. She was there for more than an hour yesterday."

"I can't promise anything." Nicholas put a hand on Mr. Taxman's shoulder. "But I'll speak with your wife."

Mr. Taxman stood straight, smoothed his tie, and responded with dignity, "Thank you, Mr. Fox. That's all I ask."

Chapter 18

A freshening breeze ruffled Nicholas's hair as we entered Saint George's Lane. He slipped into his trench coat, and I pulled on my jacket. Although no rain was falling, the rising wind gave fair warning that another April shower would soon be drenching Finch.

"You're awfully quiet," I said to Nicholas as we passed the old schoolhouse. "Are you worried about confronting Peggy?" I smiled wryly. "I don't think you'll have much trouble getting her to talk."

"You're counting on my charming ways, of course," he muttered.

I glanced at him sharply. His hair had fallen forward to hide his face, but there was no mistaking the bitterness in his voice.

"You've no idea how sick I am of my charming ways," he went on. "Has it occurred to you that I use charm as a tool, a weapon, a means of betrayal? I'm singularly adept at it. I'm so charming that I sometimes disgust myself."

I stopped short, taken aback by his out-burst. "Nicholas," I said, "what's wrong?"

"What's wrong?" He swung around to face me. "I trick people into liking me, then trick them into giving themselves away. I'm nothing but smoke and mirrors, Lori — *that's* what's wrong. Mr. Wetherhead had me pegged from the start. I'm no better than Mrs. Hooper."

I opened my mouth to object, but Nicholas cut me off.

"The secrets we've uncovered so far have been relatively harmless, but this" — he pointed toward the churchyard — "this is different. Mrs. Taxman is concealing a secret that may destroy her life, and her husband — her *husband* — is begging me to find out what it is." He thrust his hands into his coat pockets and stared angrily at the ground. "I'll do as he asks — all that charm won't go to waste — but I *don't* have to feel good about it."

I cast a cautious glance up and down the lane before asking, sotto voce, "Do you think Peggy killed Mrs. Hooper?"

"I don't know." He kicked a stone across the lane. "At the moment, I don't particularly care."

I took my lower lip between my teeth and peered up at Nicholas anxiously. Our search for truth had affected him more deeply than I'd realized. While I'd been questioning his scruples, he'd been subjecting his behavior to a scathing examination that had filled him with self-contempt. I was ashamed of myself for doubting him, and although I wanted badly to continue the search, I didn't want to do so at his expense.

"We can stop now," I offered. "We can leave Peggy to the police."

"The police?" Nicholas gave a hollow laugh. "You and I have discovered more in four days than the police have in a fortnight. They're at such a loss that they're leaning on Kit Smith, who, as far as I can tell, is the least likely suspect in the whole of England, barring the queen." He hunched his shoulders against the wind and sighed resignedly. "No. It's down to us, Lori. It's down to me."

As much as I wanted to move on to the churchyard, I knew I couldn't take another step without finding a way to console my troubled friend.

"Listen to me, Nicholas." I reached up to push his hair back from his face. "You may think you're a manipulative creep, but I beg to differ. My sons don't care for manipulative creeps, and they're crazy about you." I caught his gaze and held it. "Ruth and Louise Pym are no slouches, either, when it comes to judging a man, and they think you're the bee's knees."

"The bee's knees?" he echoed, the faint ghost of a smile playing on his lips.

"The cat's meow," I confirmed. I peered over his shoulder at the vicarage before murmuring confidentially, "And I don't know if you've noticed, but *I* think you're kind of special, too."

The ghost of a smile winked out, and I hurried on, wishing I hadn't alluded to the magnetism between us. "If you use charm to get people to talk, so what? It's better than using a truncheon."

"A truncheon would be more honest," he said heavily.

"It would also leave a lot more bruises," I retorted. "Has it occurred to you that your guilt is what makes you different from Mrs. Hooper? Unlike her, you have a conscience, and although that still small voice can be a pain in the neck at times, I'd rather be with a man who listens to it than one who tells it to shut the heck up." I took hold of his arm and gave him a gentle shake. "You're not nearly as rotten as you seem to think you are, Nicholas. Hardly anyone is."

He gripped my hand. "I wonder if you'll still feel the same way when —"

"Don't look now," I interrupted, pulling

198

my hand away, "but I think you're in for another lecture."

The door to the vicarage had opened, and Lilian Bunting had emerged. She strode to the gate, her navy-blue sweater flapping in the breeze, and eyed us both severely before telling Nicholas that he was wanted urgently on the telephone.

"Go ahead," I told him. "I'll be at the churchyard with Peggy."

Nicholas made for the vicarage and I trotted up the lane before Lilian could begin to lecture *me*.

By the time I reached Saint George's, no one was standing beside Mrs. Hooper's grave. I leaned over the low stone wall and saw that a fresh bouquet had been added to the others, but Peggy Taxman was nowhere in sight. When a flurry of fat drops spattered the bouquet's cellophane wrapping, I decided to duck into the church to avoid the coming deluge. I knew that Nicholas would have no trouble figuring out where I was.

I sprinted onto the south porch mere seconds before the downpour began in earnest. I paused to catch my breath, pleased by the near miss, before putting my shoulder to the iron-banded oak door and pushing it open. It swung inward smoothly and silently, thanks to Mr. Barlow's conscientious use of the oil can.

A soft gray light suffused the church, and the air was filled with the familiar scents of beeswax, musty prayer books, and furniture polish. I closed the door and stood listening to the rain drumming on the lead roof, then gave the bulletin board a quick once-over and scanned the pamphlets and flyers littering the table beneath it. Lilian Bunting had spent long hours revising the booklet describing Saint George's history, and I tucked a ten-pound note into the collection box, as I always did, to express my appreciation.

The drumming grew more insistent, and rivers of rain washed the leaded windows, creating weirdly watery shadows on the cold stone walls. My echoing footsteps blended with the thrumming as I wandered idly up the south aisle, rereading the memorial plaques and avoiding eye contact with the creepy medieval wall painting of Saint George battling his snaky dragon. I was about to enter the tiny Lady Chapel when I *felt* . . . something.

It was the same feeling I'd had in the vicar's study when Nicholas had crept up on me, as if an electrical field surrounding me had been disturbed. The hairs on the back of my neck prickled, gooseflesh rose on my arms, and my senses seemed to go on red alert. But it was my sixth sense that screamed most loudly, warning me of danger and urging me to flee.

I held my ground, turned, and saw a darker shadow detach itself from the gloom at the back of the church. As it passed beneath the windows, the liquid light transformed it into the formidable figure of Peggy Taxman, clad in black from head to toe, marching toward me with a stern, forbidding gleam in her pale blue eyes.

My heart pounded in time with the drumming rain, but I forced a smile and said gamely, "Hi, Peggy. Nasty weather, huh?"

"There's nastiness about," she growled, "but it's nothing to do with the weather." She came to a halt and peered past me. "Where's your lover? I thought the two of you were inseparable."

Shock rendered me speechless. Before I could recover from the bold frontal attack, Peggy had launched another.

"I've seen brazen hussies in my day, but none to match you," she ranted. "Have you no shame? Parading your fancy man under our noses, as if we were too blind or too stupid to guess what's going on. You may think you're more sophisticated than we are, with your money and your travels, but I can tell you, missy, we're worldly enough to know a T-A-R-T when we see one."

"A tart?" I felt a crazy impulse to laugh but repressed it, knowing that it would only egg Peggy on.

Peggy didn't need egging on, however. She was perfectly capable of continuing her tirade without any provocation from me.

"I don't suppose you've given a moment's thought to your poor husband, as good a man as you're ever likely to hook, working hard to support his family while you flaunt yourself behind his back." A mad glitter entered Peggy's eyes, and she gripped her black purse so tightly that her knuckles went white. "When I think of the two sweet, innocent babes you've abandoned while you're having your filthy fling, it makes me want to . . . to . . ."

Flecks of spittle were flying from Peggy's lips. Her rage was so intense as to be surreal. When she raised her fist as if to strike me, I could only watch in disbelief.

"Mrs. Taxman."

Peggy's fist froze in midair. She pivoted slowly, until she caught sight of Nicholas. He stood holding the oak door open, as if he'd only just arrived. The wind whipped his hair wildly and rain streamed from his trench coat to puddle on the tiled floor.

"*You*," snarled Peggy.

Nicholas closed the door and pushed his wet hair away from his face.

"You call yourself the vicar's nephew," Peggy began.

"I am the vicar's nephew," Nicholas said evenly. "But you and Prunella Hooper weren't old friends."

Peggy threw her shoulders back. "How dare you —"

"You and Prunella Hooper weren't old friends," Nicholas repeated, and though he raised his voice, there was nothing menacing in his manner. His face was filled with tenderness, his voice with mild regret, and he approached us with a slow, reluctant step, as though he hated himself for forcing Peggy's hand. "You didn't grow up on the same street or go to the same schools or work at the same shop — because Prunella Hooper never lived in Birmingham."

Peggy licked her lips, as if her mouth had suddenly gone dry. "I . . . I can explain."

"I wish you would," said Nicholas. "Because while my dear friend Lori has been telling her husband the truth, you've been lying to yours."

Chapter 19

The baptismal font in Saint George's Church was nearly a thousand years old. The imposing stone bowl had once been embellished with bold reliefs depicting fanciful creatures and plants, but the carvings had worn away with the passage of time, leaving only faint bumps and hollows to hint at the font's former glory.

The massive stone bowl stood atop its blunt pillar at the far end of the south aisle, in a shadowy recess opposite the Lady Chapel. Come Easter the bowl would be spilling over with lilies and drooping ferns, but the sweetly perfumed blossoms would do little to soften the font's air of austere authority.

I was here before the Church of England, it seemed to say, *and I will be here long after you have gone.*

It was a strange place to choose for a confession, but it was the place Peggy Taxman chose. Nicholas's astonishing declaration had shaken her visibly, but she was, as her husband claimed, a formidable woman. She remained on her feet long enough to stagger over to a handful of folding chairs clustered around the font, leftovers from the most recent christening. I wondered if Peggy had selected the spot for my benefit, to remind me of my "abandoned" babes, who'd both been baptized there.

When we reached the shadowy recess, Peggy seemed to run out of steam. Her face went slack; she collapsed onto a folding chair and lost her grip on her purse. The black bag opened as it fell to the floor, and a host of objects came tumbling out. Among them was a tiny stuffed animal, a brown monkey with a tan face and ears. He was faded and worn at the seams, as if he'd been with Peggy for a long, long time.

Nicholas went down on his knees to collect Peggy's things. He returned the wallet, handkerchief, date book, pens, and lipstick to the purse, but when he picked up the monkey, Peggy stretched out her hand peremptorily.

"Give him to me," she ordered.

Nicholas handed the tiny toy to her and set the purse on a vacant chair. As Peggy ran a thumb over the monkey's round and smiling face, Nicholas and I sat in chairs I'd placed opposite hers. We were close enough to hear her easily but not so close as to make her feel trapped.

The rhinestones on her pointy glasses glinted as she raised her eyes from the monkey's face to mine. "You've told your husband the truth, have you?"

I nodded. "I told Bill that I was attracted to Nicholas but that I hadn't done anything with him that I couldn't do in front of my sons. That's the truth. Whether you choose to believe it or not is up to you."

"Did Bill believe it?" she asked.

I nodded again.

Her eyes narrowed. "Angry, was he? About the attraction, I mean."

"He wasn't jumping for joy," I admitted. "But he appreciated the fact that I'd been honest with him."

"Takes courage to be honest," Peggy acknowledged, looking down at the brown monkey.

"You're a courageous woman, Mrs. Taxman." Nicholas sat with his elbows on his knees, his hands loosely clasped, a humble priest counseling a parishioner. "You're one of the most courageous women I've encountered. You've been doing your level best, under profoundly difficult circumstances, to protect your husband from a truth he might find painful."

"Poor Jasper," she murmured, "thinking so highly of me when all along . . ." Her words trailed off. She shifted slightly in her chair, pulled her coat collar more closely around her throat, and cupped the monkey in her hands.

"Prunella Hooper knew the truth," Nicholas said quietly. "She also knew why you felt you couldn't share it with your husband."

Peggy could have walked away at any moment, but Nicholas held her there with an unspoken promise of understanding, compassion, and forgiveness. His gentleness enfolded her anger and extinguished it, like a soft blanket thrown over a rising flame. Without using force of any kind, he forced her to see that, having been caught out in one lie, it was best to dispense with them all. Peggy surrendered to him without a whisper of protest.

"It started long before Prunella," she told him. "I was eight years old when my parents packed me off to Finch, to keep me safe from the blitz. I didn't go back to Birmingham till I was fifteen. I was bored to death with the country by then and raring to have a go at real life." She reached up to pat her hair, as if remembering what it had been like to be a fifteen-year-old girl taking on the big city. "Thought I knew everything there was to know, in those days. Got myself a job in a servicemen's canteen."

"A canteen?" I said. "Wasn't the war over by then?"

Peggy gave me a scornful glance. "You think soldiers run off home the minute peace is declared? Don't be daft, girl. There were millions of battle-weary men on the move all round the world and fresh ones sailing to England every day. There're still American servicemen in England, but there were more of them, in those days."

I sat back and listened, fascinated.

"There was one boy, an American fresh from training camp," Peggy went on. "He'd missed the proper war, but he came over to do his duty nonetheless. He was stationed in London, but they sent him to Birmingham to survey the reconstruction work." Peggy raised her head and stared into the middle distance while her thumb continued to stroke the monkey's face. "He came to the canteen one day. Wasn't much older than me. Had thick dark hair and hazel eyes and fine white teeth. He looked so handsome and clean in his uniform, and he was friendly, outgoing, the way Americans are. I was over the moon before he ever said boo to me."

Peggy looked down at the monkey, and I gazed at her, trying to picture the slim, bonny girl she'd once been. I imagined her gliding through a sea of panting males toward the one man who'd caught her eye, an outgoing, dark-haired boy who was far from home.

"Told him I was eighteen," Peggy said, "same as I told everyone else. Don't think he'd've looked at me twice if he'd known my real age. But he did look at me, more than twice, and after that he came to Birmingham every chance he got. Took me to funfairs and the pictures." She held up the monkey. "Won Sam for me target shooting. Named him after Uncle Sam because, he said, Uncle Sam had made monkeys of us all. He was brash like that, daring, and I loved it." Peggy smiled down at Sam. "Mark Leese, his name was. J. Mark Leese. Said he'd tell me what the J stood for after we were married."

I frowned and glanced at Nicholas before asking hesitantly, "Wasn't your first husband named Kitchen?"

"Didn't say I married Mark Leese, did I?" Peggy snapped. "Didn't get the chance. He was blown up."

I winced, and Nicholas lowered his eyes.

"Happened in London," she said gruffly.

"A team of experts was defusing an unexploded bomb. Mark was cycling past when it went off. Killed the experts. Killed him." She blew a harsh breath through her nostrils and glared at me. "You think a war is over just because a few old men say it is? There's bombs and mines and ammo dumps just waiting to carry on killing. They're still digging up bombs from the first war, over there in France and Belgium. But Mark Leese's bomb was in London, and it killed him."

The tragedy tugged at my heart across more than half a century. The war had stolen most of Peggy's childhood. It seemed unspeakably cruel that it should snatch her first love from her as well. I could think of nothing adequate to say, but beside me, Nicholas stirred.

"It was a long time ago, Mrs. Taxman," he said. "Don't you think your husband would understand if you told him that you were once in love with an American soldier?"

Peggy turned her face toward the altar to avoid Nicholas's gaze. "He might," she allowed stiffly. "But he wouldn't understand about the baby."

My jaw dropped. I looked from Peggy's shuttered face to the baptismal font and felt a chill of apprehension. "There was a baby?"

Peggy shifted Sam from one hand to the

other. "I told you. I thought I knew every-thing in those days, but I didn't. Found out I was pregnant after Mark had been blown up. My mother and father were so ashamed that they sent me north to Whitby, to live with an aunt until the baby came, so no one at home would know what kind of girl I'd turned out to be."

"Whitby," Nicholas said under his breath.

If Peggy heard him, she gave no sign.

"My auntie wanted me to stay indoors, knitting balaclavas for displaced refugees," she said. "But I was fifteen. I couldn't sit still for nine minutes, let alone nine months, so I'd sneak out while she was at church. That's how I met Prunella. . . ."

Shadows drifted across the dim recess as Peggy told her tale, her voice rising and falling with the rhythm of the rain. Prunella Hooper had been born and raised in Whitby. Her mother's boardinghouse had been two doors down from the house in which Peggy had stayed. Prunella had no-ticed Peggy's solitary strolls and decided one day to befriend her.

"She asked me in for a cup of tea," Peggy told us. "I was so bored and lonely that I nearly wept with gratitude. After that, we met every week for a cup of tea in her mother's kitchen."

The two girls soon discovered that they had much in common. They were the same age, and both had been evacuated to rural villages during the war. Peggy played it safe, at first, and stuck to stories about the years she'd spent in Finch, living above the Emporium with Mr. Harmer and his family. But Prunella proved to be a good listener, an ideal confidante, and Peggy needed desperately to talk with someone about the dashing American soldier, J. Mark Leese. It eased her heart to speak his name aloud, and before too long she'd told Prunella everything.

"Prunella wasn't a bit shocked," said Peggy. "I suppose she'd seen it all, growing up in a boardinghouse. Whatever the case, she didn't go on at me the way my auntie did, and I was grateful. She was my only friend, in those days." Peggy's gaze came to rest on the stone font. "Then the baby came. It was a boy. My auntie had it adopted and sent me home."

Her careful use of the neutral pronoun was nearly as heartbreaking as her rushed account of the baby's birth. Had she been allowed to hold her son before giving him up? Or had the child been spirited away before a bond could form between him and his young mother? I took one look at Peggy's stolid expression and couldn't bring myself to ask.

"I'd promised to keep in touch with Prunella," Peggy continued. "But after I came home I didn't want to remember Whitby, so I never answered her letters. I married Mr. Kitchen, and when he died, I came back to Finch and bought the Emporium from old Mr. Harmer. Then I married a second time. That was Jasper. Never told my husbands about Mark Leese or the baby. Never saw the need."

The need arose when Prunella Hooper sent a letter to Finch.

"It came last autumn, a week after Harvest Festival," Peggy said. "Don't know how she tracked me down. I suppose she remembered the stories I'd told her about the Emporium."

Prunella had expressed a friendly interest in Peggy's affairs and brought Peggy up-to-date on her own. In the closing paragraph Prunella had described her son's recent move to Birmingham and her own desire to come south, to be nearer her grandson. She'd asked if Peggy knew of a place that would suit her.

"Wish I'd burnt the letter," Peggy growled, "but like a fool, I wrote back. Told Prunella I couldn't help her." Her blue eyes glittered fiercely. "I didn't want her coming here, reminding me of things I wanted to forget."

It was too late, however. Prunella wrote again to say that she'd seen Crabtree Cottage listed with other holiday homes in a tourist office in Birmingham. She thought Crabtree Cottage would suit her splendidly if she and Peggy could come to terms on the rental fee.

"She asked if I had fond memories of the time we'd spent together." Peggy's voice was taut with fury. "She made it sound harmless, an old friend reminiscing, but I could read between the lines. Then she showed up, bold as brass, at the Emporium — with Jasper behind the counter! — passing herself off as an old chum from Birmingham."

"You allowed your husband to believe her," Nicholas pointed out. "You supported her story."

"Had no choice," Peggy retorted. "It was play her game or have her tell Jasper what sort of woman he'd married."

Peggy played Prunella's game. She charged Prunella nothing to live in Crabtree Cottage, and when Prunella asked for money to buy her beastly grandson the latest sneakers or the newest computer games, Peggy supplied it. Peggy defended her in public and cursed her in private. If Peggy lost her temper or threatened to rebel, Prunella brought her back in line by wondering aloud what had become of the fine baby boy Peggy had left behind in Whitby.

I glanced upward. The drumming on the roof had lessened, and dappled shadows raced across the memorial tablets, as if the sun had broken through the scudding clouds. Peggy had fallen into a meditative silence, and Nicholas appeared to be lost in thought.

As I turned Peggy's story over in my mind, I saw that it revealed more about her than perhaps she realized. I'd thought her deranged when she'd accused me of abandoning my sons, but I understood her rage better now that I knew she'd been forced to abandon her child. The strict moral code by which she judged Kit, Nicholas, and me had its roots in her own hard experience. Her love for Mark Leese had cost her dearly, and she'd been Nell Harris's age when she'd paid the price.

How could she help seeing a reflection of her vulnerable, arrogant, fifteen-year-old self in Nell? How could she restrain her hostility toward Kit if she thought he was preying on a young girl? And how could she turn a blind eye to my behavior with Nicholas when any hint of immorality would trigger memories of her own fall from grace?

"It's not just that I was in love with Mark,"

Peggy said haltingly. "It's not just that I had a baby out of wedlock. Jasper might understand about those things." The corners of her mouth trembled. "What he wouldn't understand is my giving the baby away. He always wanted a son, you see. He could've had mine if I hadn't let them . . ." She put a hand to her mouth. "I wanted to give Sam to the boy so he'd have something from his father, but they took him away before I —" A tear fell on the monkey's smiling face.

If I'd had no other reason to despise Prunella Hooper, the sight of Peggy Taxman reduced to tears would have been reason enough. Mrs. Hooper hadn't merely stuck a knife in Peggy's back. She'd twisted and turned it and thrust it in more deeply with each jab.

"Why do you put flowers on her grave?" I asked, bewildered.

Peggy cleared her throat. "My parents are gone. My auntie is gone. Prunella was my last link with the child I gave up, my last link with Mark." She wiped a tear from her cheek. "I'm grieving for Mark and my baby as much as Prunella, and I'm grieving for the girl she used to be. Prunella Hooper was a good friend to me in those days, my only friend. I'd never have believed she could turn so wicked."

Chapter 20

Peggy returned Sam to her purse and withdrew a no-nonsense plain white cotton handkerchief. She dried her eyes and wiped her glasses, tucked the handkerchief in beside Sam, and closed the purse. She seemed becalmed, as if she'd absolved herself of responsibility for whatever happened next. Having put her fate in our hands, she awaited judgment.

Nicholas ran his fingers through his damp hair and stood. He stepped up to the baptismal font and rested his palms on its rough rim. With his back to Peggy, he said, "You know what I have to ask."

"I didn't kill her," Peggy said.

"She was blackmailing you." Nicholas gave a weary, half-regretful sigh, as though he'd hoped to avoid pressuring Peggy. "She was tormenting and threatening you. You weren't with your husband on the morning of Mrs. Hooper's death. Where were you?"

"I was rearranging the display window at

the Emporium when Prunella was killed," said Peggy. "I was setting up the lawn mower and the bolt of chintz. You can ask Billy Barlow, if you like. He waved to me as he and Buster went past."

Nicholas was reluctantly relentless. "When I last spoke with you, Mrs. Taxman, you gave me the distinct impression that you *hadn't* seen Mr. Barlow and Buster. You said you'd *heard* that he'd been up early that morning. You agreed that he *might* have been walking his dog. You tried to cast suspicion onto *him*."

Peggy roused herself. "Don't you think I know how bad it looks for me?" she barked. "If some ferret-faced detective finds out about the blackmail, I'll be first in line when it comes to handing out motives. I didn't want to draw attention to myself, so I . . ." She bit her lip and squirmed as I eyed her reproachfully.

"You drew attention to other people." Nicholas finished the sentence and turned toward Peggy. His face betrayed no emotion. "You told the police to question Kit Smith, didn't you, Mrs. Taxman?"

Peggy craned her neck, as if her coat collar were choking her. "Someone had to question him. All those letters coming in, drenched in perfume. It isn't right."

"It isn't his fault," I said. "Nell's infatu-

218

ated with Kit. He's tried to discourage her, but she won't give it up." I paused before adding, "Nell's fifteen, Peggy. She thinks she knows everything there is to know."

Peggy shot a wounded glance at me. "That's why she has to be protected."

"Not from Kit," I said sternly, refusing to back down. "Kit's incapable of harming anyone but himself. You were wrong to hold him responsible for Nell's actions. You've been wrong about him from start to finish, and you owe him an apology."

"You also owe the police an explanation," Nicholas said. "You must tell them why you sent them to Anscombe Manor on a wild-goose chase."

Panic sparked in Peggy's eyes. "That would mean telling them . . . everything."

"The police will keep any information you offer confidential if it has no bearing on the crime," said Nicholas. "As will we." His expression softened, and a melancholy note entered his voice. "But I do wish you'd speak with your husband. He loves you dearly, Mrs. Taxman. It's my belief that he'll love you more dearly still when he knows what you've endured for his sake."

"I'll . . . consider it." Peggy got to her feet. "Are we finished?"

"For the time being," said Nicholas. "We

may need to speak with you again, after we've spoken with Mr. Barlow." He made a gracious half-bow. "Thank you for confiding in us, Mrs. Taxman. I hope you understand why it was necessary."

Peggy sniffed. "When murder comes through the door, privacy goes out the window," she said tartly, starting for the door. "Any fool knows that."

"Mrs. Taxman," called Nicholas.

Peggy turned.

"I nearly forgot." Nicholas took a step toward her and smiled his most engaging smile. "My aunt has called for an extraordinary meeting of the Easter vigil committee to take place tomorrow at seven in the schoolhouse. She hopes that you and Mr. Taxman will be able to attend."

"Easter vigil committee?" Peggy frowned. "First I've heard of it. Tell your aunt she can count on us, though. Jasper and I never miss committee meetings. Good day to you both — and mind how you behave. Finch is a decent village, and I intend to keep it that way." With a haughty toss of her head, she opened the oak door and left the church.

Peggy's parting shot floored me, even as it filled me with grudging admiration. The confession that had reduced her to tears hadn't come close to quenching her cantankerous spirit, and I astonished myself by hoping that nothing ever would. Though she angered and annoyed me more than anyone on earth, I knew that Finch wouldn't be Finch without its dragon.

I turned my attention to Nicholas. He was no longer smiling. He stood with his hands in his coat pockets, gazing wistfully at the iron-banded oak door.

"A pillar of the community," he murmured. "I wonder how she'll fare once her story comes out."

"Peggy will continue to breathe fire until she stops breathing altogether," I said confidently. "They broke the mold when they made her. Thank God."

Nicholas allowed himself a brief, muted chuckle.

"You okay?" I asked.

"I'm a bit overwhelmed," he replied. "Who wouldn't be? It was a moving story."

"You're the one who got it moving." I stood and stretched. I felt as if I'd been sitting in one place for hours. "How did you know that Mrs. Hooper wasn't from Birmingham? Or was it a lucky guess?"

"It wasn't a guess." Nicholas opened the door and drew a deep breath of rain-washed air. A warm, humid breeze tugged at his hair and took the edge off the chill in the church.

"The urgent telephone call I had earlier came from Aunt Lilian's goddaughter."

I scanned my memory for the reference. "The one who works at the police station?"

"That's the one. I asked her to pull up Mrs. Hooper's computer file." Nicholas took off his coat, shook residual raindrops from it, and folded it over his arm. "She discovered that Mrs. Hooper's place of birth was Whitby, not Birmingham. Mrs. Hooper lived in Yorkshire until she came to Finch."

I stared at my friend in dismay. I had no objection to receiving the odd snippet of information from Lilian Bunting's goddaughter, but I had serious reservations about pursuing those snippets intentionally. It seemed too much like spying on the police, which seemed an awful lot like something that could get him and Lilian's goddaughter arrested. Nicholas had once again behaved in a way I considered both risky and extreme.

I knew that Aunt Dimity, for one, would agree with me. She'd found it strange that Nicholas would go to such great lengths to discover who'd murdered a woman he'd never known — *a woman with whom he had no personal connection.* As Aunt Dimity's words came back to me, a startling idea took shape in my mind:

What if Nicholas *had* a personal connection?

I walked over to stand beside him in the open doorway. I studied his profile carefully before asking, "Are you . . . Peggy Taxman's son?"

A broad, authentically amused grin split Nicholas's face as he laughed out loud. "I know I'm not stripling youth, Lori — I believe your first words to me were that I was *not* a child — but do I really look as if I'm in my *fifties?*"

I did a rough calculation in my head and immediately wished I'd done so before speaking.

"Sorry," I mumbled, blushing. "Arithmetic never was my strong suit."

He was still grinning as he leaned back against the door and asked, "What on earth made you think that I might be Mrs. Taxman's long-lost son?"

I shrugged. "You seem so determined to find out who killed Mrs. Hooper. I thought for a minute that it might have been a smokescreen for finding out who your birth mother was."

"You suspect me of hidden agendas? Alas, the numbers are against you." He spoke lightly, but the momentary flash of amusement had faded from his eyes. He looked out at the graveyard. "I'm sorry, Lori. I've been a dreary companion today."

I decided then and there to clap a lid on my reservations about his illicit use of police files. Nicholas didn't need to hear a word of criticism from me. He was being hard enough on himself.

"No problem," I said easily. "I'm a woman. I can deal with mood swings."

I'd hoped the quip might restore his good humor, but his expression grew more somber still.

"I realize that my intensity disturbs you," he said, "but I need you to trust me for a little while longer. We're nearly there."

"How do you know?" I asked.

He contemplated the churchyard in silence. "The Pyms' gingerbread," he said finally. "There's only one recipient with whom we haven't spoken."

"Mr. Barlow." A flutter of excitement passed through me. "Are we going up north to track him down?"

Nicholas eyed me skeptically. "I'm not entirely convinced that your husband would be keen on the idea of us running off together."

"Probably not," I agreed, deflated. "What *are* we going to do, then?"

"We're going to wait."

Nicholas motioned for me to precede him into the south porch and followed after me, closing the door behind him. We left the porch together and ambled side by side down the gravel path toward the lych-gate. Fat clouds raced across the clearing sky as the churchyard's rain-dappled grass rippled and swayed.

I felt as restless as the rippling grass. I was no better at waiting than I was at arithmetic, but we didn't seem to have much choice. We'd discovered strong motives and weak alibis among our chief suspects but not a single witness to account for what had happened in the front window of Crabtree Cottage on the morning Pruneface Hooper had met her maker. Mr. Barlow was our last chance, and until he returned from his journey, we could do nothing but twiddle our thumbs.

As we turned into Saint George's Lane, I invited Nicholas to spend the afternoon at the cottage with me and the twins, hoping Will and Rob might succeed where I'd failed and lift his gloomy spirits. He declined, however, saying that he had to run down to London to attend to some personal business.

"Nothing's wrong, I hope," I said.

"I've a . . . doctor's appointment tomorrow

afternoon," he said, looking straight ahead. "Just routine. I scheduled it months ago. I'll be back in time for the committee meeting tomorrow evening, though." He glanced at me. "I'm counting on you to be there, too."

"Why?" I asked.

"Aunt Lilian appointed a select group of villagers to the committee," he informed me. "It's composed of the Taxmans, the Peacocks, Mrs. Pyne, Mr. Wetherhead, and Ms. Morrow."

"Miranda — ?" I broke off and smiled wryly as comprehension dawned. Either the committee had been intentionally stuffed with suspects or Lilian Bunting had decided to make a name for herself as the only vicar's wife in England to appoint a pagan to an Easter vigil committee. "Do I detect a stage manager's swagger in your walk, Mr. Fox?"

"It was Aunt Lilian's idea," he protested. "She thought it would be instructive to hold such a gathering now that you and I have, let us say, opened new lines of communication in Finch."

"I'll be there," I promised.

"Good." Nicholas flicked his hair back from his face and gazed soberly toward the square. "I expect it to be an extraordinary meeting in every sense of the word."

Chapter
21

I stopped at Anscombe Manor on the way home to have a word with Kit. I found him leaning on the paddock gate, dressed in jeans, a hooded sweatshirt, a quilted nylon vest, and muddy work boots.

His gaze was fixed on Rocinante, Nell's chestnut mare, who was galloping around the paddock and tossing her head excitedly. He was so absorbed in her boisterous antics that he didn't notice me until I rested my arms beside his on the top bar of the gate.

"Hey, Kit," I said, smiling up at him. "How're you doing?"

"Much better," he replied.

I nodded toward Rosie. "She seems happy."

"The farrier came today," he said. "She's trying out her new shoes."

While Kit watched the mare prance, I studied him. The haunted, harried look had vanished from his violet eyes. His hands rested loosely on the five-barred wooden gate, and a contented smile played upon his delicately curved lips. He seemed utterly at peace.

"You look great," I commented. "Have the nasty phone calls stopped?"

He shrugged nonchalantly. "Don't know. Emma won't allow me to answer the telephone."

"Any more visits from the police?" I asked.

He rested his chin on his arms. "Emma's solicitor has frightened them off."

"What about Nell?" I inquired. "Are you still getting letters from her?"

"She's using rosewater now," he said tranquilly. "It makes a change from lavender."

I gave him a questioning glance. "That's okay with you?"

"Look." Kit stretched out his arm and pointed across the pasture to an extremely muddy young man who'd emerged from a drainage ditch, carrying a shovel. "Annelise's brother, Lucca."

I knew Lucca. He was twenty years old, soft-spoken, hardworking, and built like Michelangelo's *David*. His tousled black curls framed a face that rivaled Kit's for beauty, and his eyes were nearly as blue as Nell's.

"Emma's hired him to help me put in a new drainage system." Kit waved to Lucca, and the young man waved back. "He'll be here for Easter and all through the summer."

"In other words," I said, "Lucca will be here when Nell's home from school."

"Precisely," said Kit.

It wasn't every stepmother who'd hire one gorgeous man to distract her stepdaughter from another, but Emma clearly felt that desperate times called for desperate measures. I gave her full marks for creativity. Her ploy might not work in the long run — Kit would be a hard act for any young man to follow — but its short-term effects were good enough for me. Emma had taken the pressure off Kit, erected a protective wall around him, and applied the balm of her own serenity to his troubled spirit. I couldn't have left my friend in better hands.

"I hope Emma's persuaded you to drop the idea of going to Norfolk," I said.

"Norfolk?" Kit swung his arm up and around me, and pulled me close to his side. "I love Anscombe Manor. I love my job. I have friends here who love me." He planted a gentle kiss on my brow. "Why would I give all of that up because of a spiteful woman and a moonstruck schoolgirl?"

As he fed my words back to me, a weight seemed to slip from my shoulders. Though I'd claimed from the start to be defending Kit, the truth was that I needed him. His sweet nature calmed and nourished my turbulent one. His essential goodness was like a beacon guiding me through a world that at times seemed very dark. If Kit had left Anscombe Manor, he would have left an irreparable hole in my soul.

I knew now that he would stay, no matter what. Whether Nicholas and I succeeded in nailing the murderer or failed miserably, Kit would go on being a part of my life. A wave of relief and gratitude filled my heart to overflowing.

"You wouldn't dare leave," I managed, fighting sudden tears, "because you know I'd come after you and drag you back by the scruff of your neck."

"My fierce angel," he murmured. He ruffled my hair, then rested his arms once more on the gate. "Emma tells me you've been wielding your burning sword on my behalf."

"Nicholas did most of the wielding," I said quickly, and told him what Nicholas and I had discovered about the good people of Finch. Kit was deeply touched to learn that so many of his neighbors had gone on believing in him despite Mrs. Hooper's wicked attempts to blacken his name.

I saved Peggy's story for last. Nicholas had promised to keep it confidential, but I refused to conceal the truth from Kit. He'd been persecuted and reviled by Peggy Taxman. He deserved to know why.

His response was characteristically magnanimous.

"What an amazing woman," he marveled. "To build a rich and rewarding life after suffering so many crushing blows . . . What fortitude."

I thought he was being a tad overgenerous and reminded him acerbically that Peggy had been willing to throw him to the wolves to save her own hide.

"She was afraid," he said simply. "She was being manipulated and threatened by a truly evil woman. I can't be angry with her."

"You can't be angry with anyone," I teased.

He smiled sweetly. "Thank you, Lori, for —"

"Don't thank me," I said abruptly. "Thank Nicholas. He was in the driver's seat. I just went along for the ride."

Kit arched an eyebrow.

"It's true," I insisted. "And I really do want you to thank him. Out loud and to his face. He needs to hear it."

Kit heard the urgency in my voice. He regarded me solemnly and put a hand to his breast.

"I will thank Nicholas," he promised.

"Out loud and to his face."

I averted my gaze, half-embarrassed by my earnestness, and saw Lucca striding across the paddock toward the gate. He greeted me warmly, asked after his sister, and requested Kit's assistance in the ditch.

I left the men to their work and went in search of Emma. She and I had a lot of catching up to do. I hadn't seen her since I'd returned from the States, and I wanted to thank her for taking such good care of Kit.

When I found her — in a closet, squatting beside a cardboard box — I scarcely recognized her. For as long as I could remember, Emma Harris had been short and generously built, with gray-blond hair hanging to her waist. Her hair scarcely touched her earlobes now, and while she was still short, her build was no longer quite so generous.

"Emma?" I said, gazing down at her. "Have you lost weight?"

"Thirty pounds," she replied, looking up from the box. "I'm going to lose twenty more before I'm satisfied. Want a kitten?"

She moved aside, and I peered over her shoulder at Katisha, Nell's calico cat, who was nursing five new additions to the family.

"The boys would love a kitten," I said, "but I'd better check with Bill first."

"Just say the word." Emma came out of the

closet, closed the door, and led the way to her large and pleasantly cluttered kitchen.

"I didn't know you were trying to lose weight," I said. "What inspired you?"

"My jodhpurs," Emma replied. "I split the seam when I went riding on Christmas Day. I took it as a sign that it was time to take my weight seriously."

She looked wonderful. As she put the kettle on and set a pair of earthenware mugs on the refectory table, I detected a fine glow to her skin, fresh energy in her step, and an unmistakable gleam of accomplishment in her blue-gray eyes.

"I like your hair," I said.

"It dries faster." Emma had a very practical turn of mind. "But enough about me. I want to know what you've been up to. I've been hearing all sorts of spicy rumors about you and the Buntings' nephew. . . ."

With a groan that was part chuckle, I sank onto a chair and began at the beginning. I gave Emma an abbreviated version of Peggy Taxman's tale, but by the time we'd finished analyzing everyone else's pecadilloes, she'd filled the two mugs with peppermint tea and placed a pot of creamed honey within my reach. I waited until she was sitting down to explain about Nicholas.

There were things you could tell a best

friend that you couldn't tell a husband or an aunt, and I told them all to Emma. I knew she wouldn't judge me or repeat my words to another living soul. She was the sort of friend Prunella Hooper had only pretended to be.

"Nicholas sounds intriguing," Emma observed, when I'd finally fallen silent. "He wouldn't appeal to you if he weren't. You like complicated men." She sipped her tea and gazed into the middle distance. "I wonder what brought on this morning's meltdown? It seems to me that there could be more to it than a tender conscience."

I drank my tea and considered Emma's comment carefully. My friend was as insightful as she was trustworthy. It wouldn't be the first time she'd picked up a cue I'd missed, and sure enough, as I reviewed the many conversations I'd had with Nicholas, a pattern began to emerge.

"Now that you mention it . . ." I tapped the rim of my mug with an index finger. "He's been on the verge of telling me something a number of times, but he's always stopped himself or been interrupted."

"Maybe it has to do with his doctor's appointment," Emma suggested. "Maybe it's been preying on his mind."

"He said it was routine," I reminded her.

"He might have been playing it down to keep you from fretting," Emma reasoned. "He sounds like someone who'd do that sort of thing."

It was exactly the sort of thing Nicholas would do. He was given to small acts of gallantry. He was the kind of man who opened doors for women, guided them around muddy puddles, wrapped blankets around them when they were chilled. I had no trouble believing that he would lie to keep me from worrying. I recalled the hesitation in his voice when he'd mentioned the appointment and felt my heart clench with dread.

"That's it." I looked at Emma in alarm. "He's sick, and he doesn't want me to know. Oh, Emma, what if he's seriously ill? What if that's why he came to see his aunt and uncle? One last visit before —"

"For heaven's sake, Lori, simmer down." Emma refilled my mug and shook her head at me, bemused. "He's not in intensive care yet. I was tossing an idea in the air. I could be completely wrong."

"What if you're right, though?" My spoon rattled agitatedly against the mug as I scooped honey into my tea. "He should have told me."

"There's probably nothing to tell." Emma rolled her eyes in exasperation. "It was just an idea, Lori. Don't worry about it." She leaned forward, her elbows on the table. "What color kitten do you think the boys will like?"

It was easy for Emma to tell me not to worry about Nicholas. She was naturally calm, cool, and collected, whereas I was absolutely none of the above. I returned home with so many knots in my stomach that I felt as if I'd gulped a mugful of macramé.

I telephoned the vicarage, but Nicholas had already left for London, where, Lilian informed me, he planned to spend the night. I considered quizzing Lilian about the state of her nephew's health but decided against it. If Nicholas had sworn her to secrecy, she wouldn't confide in me, and if he'd decided gallantly to protect her from the truth, it would be unkind to alarm her.

I spent the rest of the day and a good part of the evening afflicting Nicholas with every disease under the sun. By the time I sat down in the study to speak with Aunt Dimity, I was a bit overwrought.

Dimity allowed me to gibber hysterically for a solid five minutes before writing a single word.

Lori?

I blinked down at the page. "Huh?"

If I might redirect your attention for a moment?

"To what?" I said.

To your husband. Bill cherishes your compassionate nature, my dear, but you might want to tone down your concern lest he misinterpret it. He may not understand why you've worked yourself into such a tizzy over someone who's merely a passing acquaintance. I do, but he may not.

"You do?" I said.

I may have taken leave of this earth, Lori, but I haven't taken leave of my senses. In our recent conversations, you've expressed more interest in Nicholas than in the murder.

"That's because I care about Nicholas," I said boldly, "and I don't give a toss about Prunella Hooper. As far as I'm concerned, her death was a gift to Finch. Wait until you hear what she did to Peggy Taxman."

I've been waiting. If handwriting could be ironic, Dimity's was. I took the hint and unfolded Peggy's story in all of its poignant detail for the second time that day.

Dimity didn't respond at once. There was a long pause before her words began to scroll across the page, as if she'd needed time to reconcile her old image of Peggy the termagant with the new one of Peggy the brutalized victim.

237

Poor Mrs. Taxman. I knew there was more to her than met the eye, but I'd no idea how much more. I never would have guessed that we had so much in common. I sympathize with her more deeply than I'd ever thought possible.

I felt a pang of remorse as the real reason for Dimity's prolonged silence dawned. She, too, had lost her first love to the war. She and Peggy were bound by ties of loss and suffering I couldn't begin to comprehend.

Her burden was far greater than mine, of course, for I was never forced to give up a child. How galling it must have been for her to live under Mrs. Hooper's thumb, and how painful to have her past abused in such a way.

"I don't know how Peggy stood it," I said.

Nor do I. I find it extremely difficult to believe that a woman with her explosive temperament would submit to such a cruel form of blackmail for so long without striking out. If motive is all we have to go by, I fear that Mrs. Taxman is our most likely suspect.

"If it turns out that Peggy killed Mrs. Hooper, I'll call it justifiable homicide," I declared. "I'm reserving judgment, though, until we hear from Mr. Barlow."

A wise decision. In the meantime, try not to lose too much sleep over Nicholas's impending death. There could be other explanations for his moodiness.

"Name one," I challenged.

He could be in love with you. Sleep well, my dear.

"Sleep well?" I squeaked. I watched in mute distress as the gracefully curving lines of royal-blue ink faded from the page, then closed the journal and buried my face in my hands.

Could it be true? I asked myself. Had Nicholas fallen in love with me? I knew that he was drawn to me — he'd told me so — but he'd done nothing to suggest that his emotions were involved. When he'd said he was "not beyond temptation," I'd assumed he meant temptations of the flesh. Had I missed another cue? Had straightforward physical magnetism evolved into something deeper — something that touched his heart, disrupted his speech, filled him with melancholy?

Deeper feelings would prick at his conscience as well. He'd said only this morning that he hoped our "association" wouldn't cause trouble for me after he'd gone. He'd told me in the vicar's study that he didn't want to complicate my life. It had never crossed my mind that I might be complicating his.

While Nicholas had treated me with kid gloves, I'd played silly games. I wanted to sink through the floor when I thought of the playful, public kiss I'd given him. It had seemed like a clever joke at the time, a way of baiting my nosy neighbors. I hadn't stopped to consider its effect on Nicholas.

I felt like an unmitigated cad. When all was said and done, I could run home to my family, but Nicholas had no one to run home to — no wife, no fiancée, no girl-friend. Who would help him get over me? He didn't even own a cat.

Unrequited love could prey on a man's mind as morbidly as impending death. It suddenly occurred to me that Nicholas might have invented the doctor's appoint-ment as an excuse to put distance between himself and the unworthy object of his blighted affection.

I groaned miserably and dragged myself to bed, tormented by thoughts of love and death. Given a choice between Aunt Dim-ity's explanation of Nicholas's behavior and Emma's, I almost preferred Emma's. I could nurse Nicholas through the most dreadful of diseases, but I couldn't mend a heart that I had broken.

Chapter
22

Bill telephoned bright and early Saturday morning to let me know that, due to the demands of a particularly difficult client, he wouldn't be coming home until Sunday. I was disappointed but not surprised. Since most of Bill's clients were difficult and since he'd been away from his practice for three months, a certain number of complications were only to be expected.

I spent the rest of the day obsessing about Nicholas. I reached for the telephone a dozen times but decided each time that a phone call would be cowardly. Though I dreaded finding out that he was either heartsick or just plain sick, I felt I owed it to him to do so face-to-face.

I left the cottage early in order to help Lilian Bunting prepare the schoolhouse for the meeting and, if the opportunity presented itself, to have a private word with her nephew.

The old schoolhouse had been used as an

all-purpose meeting place since 1963, when a fire had destroyed Finch's village hall. It had once held two classrooms, but the wall dividing the two rooms had been removed to create a large open space in which the villagers conducted meetings, staged plays, and judged exhibitions related to the year's various fairs and festivals.

I'd attended many events in the schoolhouse, but none had seemed as momentous as the one that would start in less than an hour. As I parked the Rover beside the schoolyard wall, I had little doubt that the judgments passed by the select members of the Easter vigil committee would be remembered long after the winner of the Best-Flower-Arrangement-in-a-Gravy-Boat competition had been forgotten.

Work-booted butterflies romped in my stomach as I let myself in through the schoolhouse's double doors, hung my jacket on a hook in the long, narrow cloakroom, and entered the schoolroom proper. I saw at once that Lilian had preparations well in hand.

A circle of ten folding chairs sat in the middle of the room, with the refreshments table centered on the north wall. A dozen serving dishes filled with an assortment of homemade pastries had been placed on the table, along with the cheap paper napkins and the virtually indestructible cups, saucers, and teaspoons used at all community gatherings. The muted sound of running water suggested that someone was at the sink in the ladies' loo, filling the giant tea urn.

The circular seating arrangement was new to me. At every meeting I'd attended, the chairman had occupied a lofty position on the raised platform at the far end of the room, facing regimented rows of lowly committee members. I wondered if Lilian's circle had been designed to promote a more democratic spirit — or to provoke a confrontation.

I'd brought with me the Pyms' undelivered gingerbread, which I planned to distribute at the end of the meeting. I slid the boxes under the refreshments table and scanned the room, searching for some sign of Nicholas's presence. I saw none, and when the door to the ladies' bathroom opened, I hastened to give Lilian a hand lugging the heavy tea urn to the refreshments table.

"Thank you, Lori." Lilian's face was flushed from the exertion. "We keep meaning to purchase a rolling cart for this monster, but we always forget to include it in the annual budget."

"Where's the vicar?" I asked.

"I thought the meeting might be stressful for Teddy," Lilian replied, "so I sent him to spend the night at my brother's."

"What about Nicholas?" I said.

"He hasn't returned from London yet," Lilian informed me. "I expect the poor boy's trapped between lorries on the M40. The roads have become purgatorial since the government ruined the railways."

"Have you spoken with him?" I asked, fishing for details. "Did his doctor give him a clean bill of health?"

"Nicky runs five miles every morning," Lilian replied dryly. "His profession requires him to be in tiptop condition. He has nothing to fear from a routine medical examination, whereas you and I" — she paused to change her grip on the sloshing urn — "may need a chiropractor before the evening's done. Now . . . lift!"

Once we'd maneuvered the urn onto the table, Lilian plugged it in, turned it on, and stood back to survey the table. It didn't take long for her glance to fall on me.

"What a . . . striking costume," she faltered, eyeing my outfit with poorly concealed dismay. "It's so, um, homespun."

I looked down self-consciously. I'd carefully selected the shapeless gray tunic and loose-fitting black trousers in an attempt to appear as sexless as possible, for Nicholas's sake, but Lilian's pained expression suggested that I might have gone a bit overboard.

"It's comfortable," I said lamely.

"Comfort is important," Lilian agreed with a self-satisfied glance at her well-tailored tweeds.

Lilian asked me to retrieve a box of notepads and pencils from the small office at the rear of the schoolroom and to distribute one each per chair. As I scurried off to do her bidding, I congratulated myself on the subtle way in which I'd confirmed the reason for Nicholas's trip to London. I wasn't as sanguine about his health as his aunt was, but it was marginally reassuring to know that he hadn't invented the doctor's appointment as an excuse to get away from me.

I'd just finished working my way around the circle of chairs when the bells in the church tower began to chime seven o'clock. By the third *bong,* a commotion in the cloakroom signaled the arrival of the more punctual members of the Easter vigil committee.

"What in God's name are you wearing, Lori?" Peggy Taxman sailed majestically into the room, with Jasper trailing docilely in her wake. "You're not pregnant again, are you?"

I blushed crimson. "No, Peggy, I'm —"

"You've a lovely figure," Sally Pyne interrupted, marching in behind Jasper. The round-figured little woman wore a pale peach pantsuit and carried a plastic container filled with jam doughnuts, which she plonked proudly on the refreshments table. "If I had a shape like yours, Lori, I wouldn't hide it under a gray sack."

"She wasn't wearing a gray sack on the square yesterday." Dick Peacock paused in the cloakroom doorway to straighten the black brocade vest he wore over his kelly-green shirt, then made a beeline for Sally's doughnuts.

His wife, clad in corduroy trousers and a fisherman's knit sweater, followed his example but managed to delay her first bite long enough to add, "She was wearing her brown cotton jacket, Dick, which is about as alluring as the gray sack."

"All the same," Dick went on, impervious, "she looked very pretty when we saw her kissing Nicholas."

Lilian Bunting turned to me, shocked.

"Now, Dick," I began, but Christine Peacock jumped to my defense.

"It was hardly a kiss," she pointed out,

frowning at her husband. "More of a peck, really. The sort of thing you'd give a cousin."

"Too bad he's not her cousin," Dick said, waggling his eyebrows.

"He's a good friend, eh, Lori?" Sally Pyne gave me a wink as she elbowed her way to the tea urn. "A very good friend."

I didn't know where to look. I'd expected the kiss to generate gossip, but I hadn't expected it to spawn a public debate in my presence.

A throaty chuckle sounded from the cloakroom as Miranda Morrow joined the fray. Her fingers glittered with silver rings, and her flowing purple gown was covered with arcane signs embroidered in black silk.

"Scandalizing the village, Lori?" Miranda beamed at me. "I thought that was our job. Come along, George."

If George Wetherhead was abashed by Miranda's outspokenness, he didn't show it. He walked with his head held high, as if challenging his neighbors to say to his face what they'd been saying behind his back. None rose to the bait. They were too busy dissecting me.

"It's my considered opinion," ventured Jasper Taxman in his pedantic, retired-accountant's drone, "that Lori's display of affection was meant as a prank."

"She was having a bit of fun," George Wetherhead concurred. "Pulling our noses to get a rise out of us."

" 'Course she was." Christine dabbed whipped cream from the corner of her mouth. "If they were up to no good, they'd've been off snogging in the bushes, not out in the open, where everyone could see."

"Mrs. Peacock," Lilian said severely, "I'll thank you to keep a civil tongue in your head. My nephew would never dream of —"

"No need to hide in the bushes," Peggy broke in, "when they can use Wysteria Lodge, though what kind of woman would use her husband's office as a trysting place, I wouldn't like to say. Where is the young rascal, anyway?"

"I'm here."

All heads turned, and my heart skipped a beat, as Nicholas stepped into the school-room. The timing of his entrance was so contrived that I couldn't help wondering if he'd waited outside, hidden from view, until the last of our suspects had arrived.

He wore a nubby brown sweater beneath his tweed blazer and carried his trench coat over one arm. He seemed calm, but his face was very pale, and the lines around his eyes were etched more deeply than they'd been the day before. I wanted to take him aside and ask about the medical exam, but he'd already moved on to other things.

He nailed each of my tormentors with a penetrating glance. "Your suspicions about the nature of my friendship with Lori are unfounded," he said. "I wish I could say the same for your suspicions about one another."

No one spoke, and no one looked away. When Nicholas pointed to the circle of chairs, the villagers left their treats and teacups on the table and moved as if mesmerized, each taking a seat until only two places remained. Eight pairs of eyes followed Nicholas as he walked with deliberate speed to me, offered his arm, and seated me in one of the empty chairs. He elected to stand behind the other.

He draped his coat over the back of the chair, stood erect, and clasped his hands behind his back.

"You have been brought here under false pretenses," he announced without raising his voice. "There is no Easter vigil committee."

Peggy snorted, and the others relaxed, as if the familiar sound had released them from Nicholas's spell.

"Tell us something we don't know," Peggy huffed. "Easter's only a week off. Your aunt may be scatty, but she wouldn't wait till the last minute to plan a vigil."

Miranda eyed Lilian coyly. "I somehow doubt that Mrs. Bunting would ask *me* to attend such a meeting, unless, of course, she needs help elucidating Easter's pagan origins."

"We'll have none of your pagan nonsense here, thank you very much," scolded Sally Pyne. "Easter's for good, decent, Christian folk."

Miranda's nostrils flared dangerously, but Sally went on regardless.

"All I know," she said, "is that Mrs. Bunting wouldn't have invited me without having her husband apologize to me first." She shook a finger at Lilian. "If the vicar thinks I'm going to forget —"

"No one thinks you're going to forget," George Wetherhead muttered, clutching his head. "We'll be hearing about those dratted flowers from now until doomsday."

"Ladies, gentlemen, please." Lilian tapped her notepad with her pencil. "My husband will be away from home until tomorrow morning, but I'm sure that, when he returns, he will offer an apology to Mrs. Pyne. He truly regrets his decision regarding the Easter flowers. Now, if we might come to order?"

"How can we come to order with the chairs in a circle?" Peggy objected. "There's no way of telling who's chairwoman."

"I'm chairwoman," Lilian said crisply. "And I'm giving my nephew the floor. Nicky?"

Nicholas rested his hands on the back of the empty chair and looked from one face to the next around the circle. Christine Peacock sat beside Lilian, with Dick to her right. After Dick came Peggy Taxman, Jasper Taxman, Sally Pyne, George Wetherhead, and Miranda Morrow. Nicholas stood between Miranda and me.

"Gossip is an inevitable fact of community life," he began. "Wherever two or more are gathered, someone will talk behind someone else's back."

"True enough," said Dick, stroking his goatee complacently.

"Nothing wrong with a bit of tittle-tattle," Sally commented.

"I'd agree with you, Mrs. Pyne, under normal circumstances," said Nicholas, "but circumstances in Finch are far from normal. A murder has taken place. Destructive rumors abound. Law-abiding citizens refuse to help the police."

"There's no need to involve the police," Sally declared. "Finch takes care of its own."

"Does it?" Nicholas saw the opening and darted through it. "Were you taking care of Mr. Peacock when you told me he'd been on the square at the time of Mrs. Hooper's death?"

Dick's hand froze midstroke, and his eyes slid toward Sally Pyne. "Telling tales out of school, are we, Sally?"

"Don't get your knickers in a twist, Dick," Peggy Taxman chided. She looked askance at Nicholas. "We know what Dick's doing on the square every Thursday morning, and it isn't smacking women in the head."

"That's right," Sally said, fiddling nervously with her pencil. "Mr. Peacock's a businessman, same as the rest of us, and if he needs to cut corners to make ends meet, we're not going to turn him in."

"What the inland revenue don't know won't hurt it," George Wetherhead pronounced.

Dick tore his hostile gaze away from Sally and looked at George in confusion. "Inland revenue? What's the inland revenue got to do with it?"

Mr. Wetherhead seemed flustered by the question, so Miranda took over for him.

"Come now, Mr. Peacock," she said smoothly. "You're among friends. If you choose to deal in duty-free goods —"

"Smuggled booze," Sally corrected.

"— it's no one's business but yours," Miranda concluded.

Nicholas eased himself into his chair and let the conversation flow unchecked. He'd gotten the ball rolling and seemed content to wait and see where it would stop.

"I'm afraid that's not quite true, Miranda," Lilian was saying. "Tax evasion is a criminal offense, and I, for one, cannot condone it. Breaking the law —"

"We haven't broken any law," Dick protested. "I've never sold a drop of smuggled liquor."

Peggy's eyes narrowed. "You can lie to the police, Dick, but don't lie to us."

"I'm not lying," Dick insisted.

"What's the van man dropping off, then?" Sally demanded. "Easter eggs?"

"Duty-free Easter eggs?" Miranda purred.

"We've all seen him, Dick," Peggy said sternly, "so you may as well —"

"For heaven's sake, leave Dick alone!" Christine flung her arm across her husband as if to protect him from the onslaught. "It's sausages, alright? *Sausages!*"

The inquisition came to a screeching halt as we looked blankly at Dick's wife.

"Pardon?" said Lilian.

"It's sausages," Christine repeated sullenly. She dropped her arm, stared down at her notepad, and colored to her roots. "Everyone thinks I make my own, but the sight of blood makes me dizzy, so I buy them from a pig farmer near Evesham. Dick arranged to have them delivered on the sly so no one would know they're not home-made."

A deflated silence followed Christine's revelation.

"Not an old family recipe?" Sally inquired.

"No," Christine admitted, shamefaced. "Not from *my* family, at any rate."

"They're awfully good sausages," I offered.

"I wouldn't use 'em if they weren't," Christine snapped. "I do have standards, you know."

"A pity they don't include telling the truth," Miranda said under her breath, but the circle was too small to allow any comment to go unremarked.

Dick's chair creaked alarmingly as he sat bolt upright, his eyes flashing. "If it's truth you want, Ms. Morrow, you might try telling it yourself. You're among friends," he sneered, "so I'm sure you won't mind telling us what kind of rumpty-tumpty you and George have been getting up to."

An even more deflated silence followed Miranda's blithe and clinical description of

George Wetherhead's ongoing program of physical therapy. Although murmurs of "Good for you, George" went round the circle, they sounded halfhearted at best. The villagers patently preferred the romantic fables they'd concocted to the mundane truth. Sausages and therapeutic massages couldn't hold a candle to smuggled booze and illicit rumpty-tumpty.

"Seems a silly way to go about it," Sally grumbled, voicing the unspoken consensus. "Leave it to a witch to go all secretive when there's no need. They call it being mysterious, but I'd call it sneaky."

I held my breath, anticipating an explosion. It was the second time in less than twenty minutes that Sally had insulted Miranda Morrow's way of life. I half-expected Sally to vanish in a puff of peach-colored smoke.

"Witches aren't the only ones who like to keep secrets, though, are they, Mrs. Pyne?" Miranda Morrow smiled, but her eyes were like chips of ice. "How did you know where Dick was on the morning of Mrs. Hooper's death? Up early, were you? Out and about?"

Sally flushed. "I . . . I don't know what you mean."

"Of course you do, Mrs. Pyne, but I won't give you away. You know how good we witches are at keeping secrets." Miranda stretched her arms out and gazed languorously at the silver rings adorning her fingers. "I'll never tell a soul that I saw you that morning, *coming out of Crabtree Cottage.*"

Chapter
23

A collective gasp should have gone up from the group, but the only ones to gasp were Lilian and me. Nicholas sat motionless, staring at the floor, while the others shuffled their feet and looked everywhere but at Sally.

Sally looked daggers at Miranda. "Who's going to believe *you?*"

Miranda batted her eyelashes. "You needn't take a pagan's word for it," she said. "George is a good, decent Christian, and he saw you, too."

"Miranda was leaving my place," the little man piped up loyally, "when Sally came tiptoeing out of Crabtree Cottage. We both stepped back inside so she wouldn't see us."

"It was nearly six o'clock," Miranda added. "The sun was hidden by clouds, but there was enough light for us to recognize Mrs. Pyne." She twirled a lock of strawberry-blond hair around her finger. "Why so tense, Mrs. Pyne? I'm sure it was merely a social call. To discuss the fine art of flower arranging, perhaps?"

Sally's pencil snapped in two.

"You've made your point, Ms. Morrow." Nicholas's soft voice intervened. "There's no need to be unkind." He raised his head to gaze levelly at Sally Pyne. One by one, the others followed suit.

Sally placed the broken pencil and her notepad on the floor, planted her fists on her thighs, and declared, "I want to make one thing plain: Pruneface was dead when I got there."

"Y-yes, Mrs. Pyne," Lilian faltered. The vicar's wife was clearly rattled. "Of course she was. And I'm sure you can offer us a perfectly reasonable explanation for failing to notify the police when you found her, um, body."

"Everyone knew that I held a grudge against Pruneface on account of the baptismal font," Sally said. "I thought it would look suspicious if it was me who found her."

"So you left it to me," Peggy growled.

"It was a rotten thing to do, Peggy," Sally said humbly, "but I knew you'd be along to collect the rent, and I didn't think it'd matter so much if you found her. You were her chum. No one would suspect you of doing her in."

Peggy glanced furtively at Nicholas and clamped her mouth shut.

"Why did you go there in the first place?" asked Christine.

"Believe it or not," Sally replied, "I went to discuss flower arranging. . . ."

Sally had spent a restless night fretting about the Easter display. She knew that Pruneface had snatched the project from her out of spite, and she feared that Pruneface might make a hash of it.

"I was afraid she might try to foist some god-awful modern nonsense on us," Sally explained. "You know the sort of thing — a bare branch and a pile of pebbles to symbolize God alone knows what."

"Teddy wouldn't have allowed it," Lilian protested indignantly.

Sally gave her a jaundiced look. "That's as may be," she allowed with exaggerated politeness, "but I couldn't risk it. The font's always been my responsibility, so I thought I'd have a chat with Pruneface, to let her know that Finch isn't the sort of place that takes kindly to experiments. . . ."

Sally had risen at five o'clock to make herself a cup of tea and thus had witnessed the bustle of activity on the square. She'd seen Dick unloading the gray van, Peggy rearranging the Emporium's display window, and Mr. Barlow walking Buster. She'd taken particular note of Pruneface spying on Dick Peacock from the front window of Crabtree Cottage.

"I knew she was awake," Sally said, "so I told myself, No time like the present. After I got dressed and had a bite to eat, I nipped across the square."

"What time was it when you reached her house?" I asked.

"A quarter to six," Sally replied. "The church bells were ringing the quarter hour when I knocked."

I jotted *5–5:45* on my notepad.

"I knocked several times, good and loud," Sally continued, "and when Pruneface didn't come to the door, I got upset. I thought she was snubbing me again, so I pushed the door open and invited myself in."

The schoolroom was so quiet that I could hear the tap dripping in the ladies' bathroom. Nicholas sat very still, but it was the stillness of self-absorption rather than watchfulness. He seemed distant and withdrawn, detached not only from me but from the group at large, as if preoccupied by something far more troubling than the murder we'd spent all week investigating.

"I called her name," Sally went on, "and

when she didn't answer, I thought she might have fallen ill or hurt herself." Sally regarded us pugnaciously. "I didn't care for the woman, but I know what it's like to live alone, and I couldn't leave without making sure she was alright."

George Wetherhead nodded, and there was no trace of mockery in Miranda's somber expression. Like Sally, they knew the hazards of living alone.

"I went into the front parlor," said Sally, "and there she was, stretched out beneath those red geraniums . . . dead. I thought she'd had a stroke" — Sally took a shaky breath — "till I saw the blood. It gave me a queer turn, I can tell you."

Her eyes glazed briefly, and the rest of us shuddered, as if we'd each glimpsed those red geraniums reflected in Mrs. Hooper's blood.

Sally ran a hand through her hair. "That's when I realized how suspicious it would look for me to be there. So I made sure the coast was clear and nipped back to the tearoom."

"You could have rung the police anonymously," said Lilian.

"And have my number recorded? I might as well have turned myself in." Sally lifted her chin determinedly. "I don't imagine any of you will believe me, but it's the God's truth. Pruneface Hooper was dead when I found her."

I waited for Nicholas to speak, but he remained lost in his own thoughts.

"You said you saw Mr. Barlow walking Buster," I ventured. "Did you see him enter Crabtree Cottage?"

Sally shook her head. "He walked Buster to the war memorial and tossed that silly rubber ball a few times. He let out a big laugh once, like he does when Buster makes a good catch; then he went home. Ten minutes later, he and Buster hopped into the car and took off. I didn't see him go into the cottage."

I referred to my scanty notes. If Sally was telling the truth, Mrs. Hooper had been killed between five and five forty-five in the morning, when nearly everyone present had been awake, dressed, and smarting under Mrs. Hooper's lash.

"Sally," I said, "did you see anyone enter or leave Crabtree Cottage *before* you went there?"

"I wasn't watching the whole time," Sally answered. "I suppose someone could've gone in without my noticing, but it would've taken some pretty fancy footwork for them to get out again."

"Miranda and I didn't see anyone but Sally," George offered.

Lilian sat forward. "Did any of you see anyone other than Mrs. Pyne enter or leave Crabtree Cottage on the morning in question?"

The villagers quailed under her stern, schoolmarmish gaze, and after a moment's discomfited silence, Dick spoke up.

"I saw Sally," he said reluctantly. "I was scrubbing glasses in the pub when she made her dash back to the tearoom."

"Dick told me he'd seen her," Christine admitted.

"Christine passed it on to me," Peggy informed us.

"My wife confided in me, of course," Jasper added.

"You *all* knew, yet *not one* of you saw fit to share this very pertinent information with the authorities?" Lilian clucked her tongue in disapproval.

"It was nothing to do with them, Mrs. Bunting," said Dick. "None of us thought Sally would kill someone over the ruddy baptismal font. Even if she had, I wouldn't've blamed her overmuch. Mrs. Hooper was a small-minded, interfering old crow who caused nothing but misery. She deserved a clout in the head."

"I didn't shed a tear when I found her," Sally acknowledged. She smiled ruefully at Dick. "To be honest, I was convinced you'd smacked her — to keep her from turning you in to the inland revenue. And I didn't blame you, either."

"Decent of you, Sally." Dick nodded toward George Wetherhead. "My money was on old George. I thought he'd whacked her with his crutch to keep her from blabbing about his affair with Miranda."

"Did you really?" George's face lit with delight. "I didn't kill Pruneface, Dick, but it was kind of you to think of me."

"My pleasure," said Dick with a friendly nod.

I didn't know whether to be amused or disgusted by the abrupt change in atmosphere. The tense confrontation engineered by Lilian Bunting had suddenly turned into a convivial gathering of neighbors eager to clear up a slight misunderstanding. Murder accusations weren't hurled, but tossed lightly between suspects, and the accused responded not with howls of protest but with good-humored, low-key denials.

"I have to admit that I thought Miranda might've had a hand in Pruneface's death," George said, going with the flow. "I'm sure you've heard the lies she concocted about

Miranda's medicinal herbs."

The villagers' hesitant nods and sidelong glances suggested that although they were less certain than George that all of Miranda's herbs were strictly medicinal, they'd still rather side with her than with Pruneface.

"The wretched woman threatened to turn Miranda in to the drug squad," George went on. "I would've understood if Miranda had thumped her."

"You sweet creature," said Miranda, patting George's knee. "I was out of patience with Mrs. Hooper, but I don't believe in violent retribution. I was quite willing to leave her fate in the hands of the goddess."

"Let's see now . . ." Dick licked his pencil and applied it to his notepad. "I didn't smash her head in, nor did my wife, and Sally, George, and Miranda claim they didn't. So that leaves . . ." He circled three names on his scribbled list. "Mr. Barlow, Jasper, and Peggy."

"I'd cross Peggy off the list if I were you," Sally advised. "Why would she knock off an old chum?"

"You'd have to ask her," Miranda murmured.

I was about to step in when I was distracted by a faint, familiar yapping coming from outside the schoolhouse. A cool breeze fluttered the paper napkins on the refreshments table as the outer doors opened. Claws skittered on the cloakroom floor, and Buster bounced into the room, followed closely by Mr. Barlow.

As the terrier gamboled merrily around the circle, greeting all and sundry, a second man entered the room. He was in his mid-fifties, I guessed, with a sprinkling of gray in his thick dark hair. He scanned the faces in the room anxiously, as if hoping to find someone he knew. When his eyes met Peggy Taxman's, his chest heaved.

"Mrs. Taxman?" he said.

"M-Mark?" Peggy gasped, and toppled slowly from her chair in a dead faint.

Chapter
24

If Jasper hadn't broken her fall, Peggy would have broken her head. The stranger rushed forward to help Jasper prop her up, and Mr. Barlow seized Buster's collar to keep the frisky terrier from licking Peggy's face. Lilian fetched a cup of water from the ladies' bathroom, dampened a paper napkin, and applied it to Peggy's temples.

While everyone else milled around Peggy, I kept an eye on Nicholas. The commotion had broken his trance. He blinked, as if emerging from a deep sleep, and stiffened when he caught sight of Mr. Barlow. He turned toward me, but before he could say a word, Peggy's eyelids fluttered open.

She raised a trembling hand to touch the stranger's face. He gazed down at her tenderly and nodded.

"That's right, Mrs. Taxman," he said. "I'm your son."

Everyone froze. Even Buster stopped squirming and pointed his twitching nose in Peggy's direction.

A sob caught in Peggy's throat. "Y-your name," she stammered. "What did they call you?"

"Harry," he replied. "Harry Mappin, after my father."

Peggy pushed herself into a sitting position and said fiercely, "Your father's name was *J. Mark Leese,* and don't you forget it."

"No, ma'am," Harry said gently. "I won't."

Lilian Bunting applied the dampened napkin to her own temples as she stood. She touched Sally's arm, then Miranda's, and the milling villagers gradually cleared a space around the tableau on the floor.

"Welcome to Finch, Mr. Mappin," Lilian said with astonishing aplomb. "May I offer you a cup of tea?"

"We're going home," Peggy barked. She allowed Jasper and Harry to haul her to her feet, straightened her dress, and glared defiantly at her neighbors. "I had a baby when I was a girl, and I gave him up for adoption. There you have it! And that's all you're going to get till I've had a chance to speak with my husband and m-my boy." She hooked one hand through Jasper's arm, and the other through Harry's, and marched them out of the schoolhouse without a backward glance.

One by one, the villagers returned to their chairs. Sally Pyne opened her mouth, but closed it again without emitting a syllable. Miranda Morrow studied her silver rings, Christine Peacock scratched her head, and George Wetherhead appeared to be thoroughly at sea. Dick Peacock watched Mr. Barlow, who was looking from Lilian to Nicholas as if awaiting instructions.

Nicholas was the first to break the silence. "Mr. Barlow," he said, "would you be so kind as to tell us where you've been and what you've been doing?"

Mr. Barlow released Buster's collar, swung Jasper Taxman's chair around, and straddled it, his arms folded across the back. Buster curled alertly at his feet.

"I never pretended to like Mrs. Hooper," he said gruffly. "I know trouble when I see it, and Mrs. Hooper was trouble with a capital T. I watched her stirring her little wasps' nests all winter long, and when she kicked my pup, I decided that enough was enough. If she wouldn't leave Finch voluntarily, I'd find a way to make her go. That's why I went to Birmingham, to have a chat with that son of hers."

"You told us you were going up north to visit family," said Sally.

"That came later," said Mr. Barlow, "after

269

I learned from Mrs. Hooper's son that his mother never lived in Birmingham."

The villagers exchanged glances, then sat forward, their chins in their hands, enraptured by the new, exciting tidbit Mr. Barlow had unearthed.

"Prunella Hooper was from Whitby," said Mr. Barlow. "That's where she met Peggy Taxman."

"Peggy said —" Christine began, but Mr. Barlow would brook no further interruptions.

"Peggy lied," he said bluntly. "You and I know that Peggy Taxman never lies, even when we wish she would, so it struck me as strange that she'd tell a lie about Mrs. Hooper. Then it struck me that maybe Mrs. Hooper had invented the lie and forced Peggy to go along with it."

Sally grunted. "I can't see anyone forcing Peggy to do anything."

"What if Mrs. Hooper had something on Peggy?" Dick interjected. "Some secret Peggy didn't want us to know."

"Such as an illegitimate child?" Miranda suggested, gazing toward the cloakroom.

"You want me to tell the story?" Mr. Barlow asked with a touch of petulance. "Or do you want to go on guessing?"

"Forgive us, Mr. Barlow," Lilian said

hastily. "Please continue."

"I was born near Whitby, in Scarborough," he said. "I still have family up there, so I decided to go see 'em. I figured they might've heard of Mrs. Hooper. A woman like that always leaves a trail. . . ."

Mr. Barlow's relatives had heard of Mrs. Hooper. What's more, they'd been able to put him in touch with several of her former neighbors, classmates, and coworkers, some of whom had been willing to describe the havoc she'd wrought in their lives.

"Leopards don't change their spots," said Mr. Barlow. "Prunella Hooper pulled the same nasty tricks in Whitby that she pulled in Finch. She spied on people, eavesdropped, started rumors, made threats, spread lies. She befriended folk, then waited for her chance to stab 'em in the back. That's what she did to Peggy. . . ."

The trail of contacts had led Mr. Barlow to an old people's home near Whitby, where he'd struck gold in the form of an elderly resident called Mick Shuttleworth.

"Old Mick had lived in the boardinghouse run by Prunella Hooper's mother," said Mr. Barlow. "He was there after the war, when Prunella befriended a pregnant girl who was staying with an aunt just up the street. Mick still remembered the girl's name — Peggy

Stanton." He nodded to Lilian. "Church records'll confirm that Stanton was Peggy Taxman's maiden name."

Mick Shuttleworth had seen Prunella in action, stirring wasps' nests in the boardinghouse, and he knew that she would cause young Peggy grief. He'd tried to warn Peggy to steer clear of Prunella, but Peggy wouldn't hear a word said against her friend. When Prunella got wind of Mick's efforts, she forced him to leave the boardinghouse.

"Mick wouldn't say what lies she spread about him," Mr. Barlow said grimly, "but I imagine they were along the same lines as her lies about Kit and Nell. It made the old gentleman's blood boil to think of it, all these fifty years later."

Mick had kept an eye on Peggy even after he'd left the boardinghouse, and when she'd given birth, he'd made it his business to find out where the baby had gone in case Peggy ever came looking for her child.

"That's how I found Harry Mappin," said Mr. Barlow. "He'd been given to a couple in Pickering. Harry knew he'd been adopted, but he was one of thousands of wartime babies whose records were shifted from pillar to post. He'd had no luck tracing his birth mother."

Lilian looked at Mr. Barlow with a faint air

272

of reproof. "Was it necessary to bring Mr. Mappin here?" she asked. "Mrs. Taxman might have appreciated a word of warning."

"Harry wouldn't wait," said Mr. Barlow. "And I can't say that I blame him."

Lilian remained doubtful. "But to introduce him so publicly —"

"Isn't that what you wanted?" Mr. Barlow pushed himself up from his chair. "It's like you said to me before I left, Mrs. Bunting: There've been too many secrets floating around this village, too many people being hurt by half-truths. It was time to clear the air."

A murmur of assent filled the schoolhouse, but Miranda didn't add her voice to it.

"Have we cleared it, though?" she mused aloud. "I wonder . . ."

Dick stroked his goatee. "The way I see it," he said, "Pruneface threatened to tattle about Harry unless Peggy sided with her against us."

"There's more to it than that, isn't there, Nicholas?" When Nicholas didn't reply, Miranda looked at me. "Were you able to confirm my suspicions, Lori? You've been poking and prying so zealously. You must have learned something by now."

I glanced uncertainly at Nicholas. "I, uh,

don't think this is the time or place to —"

"I'm sorry, Lori, but Mr. Barlow is quite right," Lilian interrupted. "It must all come out, here and now. I would urge you to share with us whatever you and Nicky have learned."

"I can't," I said. "Peggy spoke to us in confidence. I won't betray her trust."

"Nicky?" said Lilian.

"I'll leave it to Ms. Morrow," Nicholas said softly. "Her conclusions were essentially correct."

Miranda wasted no time in telling the others about the argument she'd overheard at the Emporium.

"The quarrel led me to believe that Mrs. Hooper wasn't paying one cent in rental fees to Peggy," Miranda concluded, "and that Peggy was giving her money from time to time, to keep her mouth shut."

"Now we know why," Dick commented. "Who would've thought it of Peggy? Having a baby out of wedlock when she's always telling us to mind our morals."

"Maybe that's why she tells us to mind our morals," said Christine. "She's seen what happens to those who don't."

"You're missing the point." Sally Pyne jumped to her feet, too overcome by indignation to remain seated. "It was nobody's business but hers. Pruneface had no right to hold it over her. Poor old Peggy . . ." She ground her teeth. "It doesn't bear thinking about."

"We must think about it, though," Christine said gravely. "You know what I mean. If anyone had a motive to kill Pruneface, it was Peggy."

"So what if she did?" retorted Sally.

"I'd vote to pin a medal on her," George Wetherhead chimed in.

Mr. Barlow put two fingers in his mouth and whistled shrilly, silencing the chatter.

"Listen up," he said. "Peggy Taxman didn't kill Pruneface Hooper."

"How do you know?" Sally asked.

"I was there when it happened, that's how." Mr. Barlow glanced at Nicholas. "I saw Pruneface Hooper die."

My jaw dropped, Dick sputtered, and Sally's eyes nearly popped out of her head, but Nicholas didn't turn a hair.

"Pardon?" Christine said weakly.

"You heard me," said Mr. Barlow. "I'm surprised you haven't been told about it already."

Nicholas bowed his head. "Mr. Barlow," he murmured, "if you would be so kind as to explain . . . ?"

"Very well." Mr. Barlow waited until Sally

had resumed her seat before speaking. "When I took Buster for his run that morning, I spotted Pruneface standing in her usual place, snooping on Dick. She had a curling iron in one hand, and she was holding back one of those hanging plants with the other so she could get a clearer view of the pub." He demonstrated Mrs. Hooper's stance, then went on.

"Buster's barking must've startled her because the next thing I knew, she let go of the plant. It swung across and whacked her" — he touched the place on his head where Nicholas had touched me — "here. She went down like she'd been poleaxed."

Christine gaped at Mr. Barlow. "Pruneface Hooper was killed by a *flowerpot?*"

"I'd say she killed herself," Mr. Barlow opined, "but a flowerpot's what bashed her head in."

"Why didn't you report it?" asked Sally.

"I didn't know she was dead," said Mr. Barlow. "I thought the flowerpot had knocked her silly, but I didn't know it had killed her. I laughed when she went down."

"I heard you," Sally said faintly.

Mr. Barlow bent to fondle Buster's ears. "I told myself that Buster had gotten his own back on her and that she deserved a bump on the head for kicking him. That's what I told the police when they tracked me down yesterday."

Sally put a hand to her forehead. "The police have known the truth since yesterday?"

"If they'd done their job right, they'd've known it a good deal sooner," said Mr. Barlow. "Isn't that right, Detective-Sergeant Fox?"

A profound hush fell over the room as everyone turned to look at Nicholas.

He closed his eyes. "Yes, Mr. Barlow. If we'd done our job right, we'd have closed the case last week."

Chapter
25

Miranda clapped her hands. "I knew it!" she exclaimed. "Auras never lie. I did invite you to bring the drug squad with you to tea, if you recall, Detective-Sergeant."

Dick eyed me reproachfully. "You brought a copper into my pub and didn't bother to tell me?"

I sensed Nicholas's gaze on me but refused to look at him. "I didn't know he was a copper, Dick. He didn't tell me."

Sally looked thunderstruck. "The two of you, thick as thieves, and he never told you he was a policeman? Well, I never . . ."

Christine addressed Lilian. "You must have known. He's your nephew — isn't he?"

"Don't be silly, Christine," said Lilian. "Of course Nicky's my nephew, and I'm well aware of his profession. When he came to stay, I asked him to —" She broke off as Nicholas got to his feet and strode out of the schoolhouse. "Lori," she said worriedly, "go after him. *Please.*"

I felt so hurt and humiliated that I was tempted to turn a deaf ear to her plea. Nicholas had lied to me, used me, and left me to face my neighbors without a word of explanation. He'd demanded the truth from everyone else, but he hadn't had the decency to tell it to me.

Worst of all, he'd made me feel stupid. I'd noted his observation skills and his polished interrogation technique — I'd even described his good cop/bad cop routine to Aunt Dimity — but I hadn't suspected for one minute that he might actually be a cop. He'd telegraphed his occupation in a hundred different ways, but although I'd seen the pieces, I'd been too thickheaded to see the bigger picture.

I'd trusted Nicholas, and in return he'd made a fool of me. If he hadn't left his trench coat behind, I might have climbed into my Rover and gone home to sulk.

But I couldn't ignore the lightning bolt that illuminated the schoolhouse windows. When it was followed by a crash of thunder and a sudden, heavy downpour, I let out an aggrieved sigh, snatched the black trench coat from the back of the chair, and raced out of the schoolhouse, grabbing my own jacket on the way.

I saw Nicholas at once, a solitary figure

silhouetted against Miranda's hedge by a second lightning flash. He stood with his head in his hands, unmoving, despite the driving rain.

"Nicholas!" I shouted, running up Saint George's Lane. "You idiot!" I came to a halt before him, panting. "You forgot your coat."

His arms fell to his sides, but he said nothing. Rain streamed from his face and hair, and his tweed blazer was soaked through, but he made no effort to take the trench coat from me.

I threw it around his shoulders and glared at him. "Planning to stand here all night?"

Still he said nothing.

"Are you *trying* to catch pneumonia?" I demanded truculently. "You're crazy if you think I'll let you off the hook that easily."

He made no reply, but gazed down at me with such a look of hollow-eyed despair that my anger leached away, to be replaced by uneasiness.

"Nicholas?" I said, wiping the rain from his face. "Nicholas, come with me."

I took his hand as if he were a child and led him into the vicarage, where I knew we wouldn't be disturbed. The vicar was spending the night with Lilian's brother, and Lilian would be fully occupied, answering questions about her nephew. If Peggy, Jasper, and

Harry returned to the schoolhouse, the session might drag on for hours.

Nicholas was as docile as a lamb. I threw our wet coats onto a chair in the foyer, helped him out of his blazer, and held his arm while he slipped his shoes off. He let me take him to the green velvet sofa in the vicar's study, where I got a fire going, toweled his hair, and wrapped him in a blanket. I considered making cocoa, but I was afraid to leave him alone for too long, so I added another stick of wood to the fire and sat beside him on the sofa.

I let the silence linger before asking solemnly: "Are you dying?"

Nicholas's laugh twisted into a sob. He pulled his hands free of the blanket and wiped his eyes. "I may be having a nervous breakdown, Lori, but I don't seem to be dying."

I looked up at him. "Are you really a policeman?"

"I don't know what I am," he replied. "But I did at one time work undercover for the drug squad. As Ms. Morrow is so fond of pointing out, auras never lie." He squinted vaguely at the fire. "I can't think why she didn't give me away."

"Haven't you heard? Witches like to keep secrets." I looked down at the threadbare

Turkish carpet. "Can you tell me about this nervous breakdown?"

He hunched forward, pulling the blanket around him more closely, and stared unblinking into the fire for a long time before he spoke.

"I had . . . a partner," he began. "His name was Alex Layton. Our last case" — he swallowed hard — "ended badly."

He was shivering. I reached over to gently stroke his back.

"It ended badly," he repeated. His voice was barely above a whisper. "Someone slipped up, our covers were blown, and the bad guys got to us before we could pull out. They knocked me about and shot me full of dope but kept me conscious long enough to watch as they beat Alex to death."

His sea-green eyes had lost their luster, gleaming dully beneath a glaze of tears. Lightning flashed and thunder rolled and rain crashed against the French doors, but Nicholas seemed aware of nothing but the nightmare visions he alone could see writhing in the flames.

"I awoke in hospital. I'd been rescued and revived, but no one could save Alex. The human skull is so fragile in places that even a flowerpot can break it." He bowed his head and pressed the heel of his hand to his brow. "Imagine what a length of pipe can do."

My heart ached for him so badly that I could scarcely breathe. I remembered how he'd jerked his hand away after showing me where Mrs. Hooper had been struck. Had he seen his partner's face for one brief moment, relived the horror of his partner's death?

"When I recovered," he said softly, "they put me on light duties, teaching self-defense to new recruits." He touched my leg. "It wasn't all lies."

"It's okay," I said. "It doesn't matter."

He closed his eyes. "When I put my fist through one wall too many, they gave me three months' leave without the option. I spent the first month drunk, the second in counselors' offices, and the third getting myself back in shape. I came to Finch to rest up before my final meeting with the medical board."

The doctor's appointment, I thought. He'd had to face the medical board only a few hours before he'd faced the villagers.

"When I first arrived in Finch," he said, "Aunt Lilian asked me to look into the circumstances surrounding Mrs. Hooper's death. She told me there was bad blood in the village and that it needed to be purged."

"Does she know about Alex?" I asked.

He shook his head. "It's not the sort of thing one tells one's aunt. It's not the sort of thing one talks about at all, if one can avoid it."

I put my arm around him. "But you couldn't refuse your aunt's request without telling her why."

"She's so proud of me." He sighed. "Me and my charm. The villagers would never suspect Mrs. Bunting's charming nephew of being a copper. She said you mustn't know, either, because you'd give me away. Not intentionally," he added, and turned to cup my chin in his hand. "You have many gifts, Lori, but concealing your thoughts isn't one of them."

"Maybe you can coach me," I said ruefully. "Teach me Zen and the art of playing poker."

"I wouldn't change you for the world." Nicholas touched his forehead to mine, then turned back to the fire. He'd stopped shivering, but his face remained shadowed with despair.

"I thought I could handle the villagers," he said, "but their callousness got to me. They spoke constantly of *whacking* Mrs. Hooper, *clouting* her, *thumping* her, *smashing* her head in — cavalierly, without remorse, until I couldn't tell the difference between them and the thugs who'd killed Alex. If you hadn't been with me, I might've put my fist through a few more walls."

I reached for his hand and gazed down at the scarred, misshapen knuckles. They bore mute witness to the damage his soul had sustained.

"I almost wish you had punched a few walls," I said.

He looked at me questioningly.

"I wish you hadn't kept your feelings bottled up," I told him. "I wish you'd shouted, screamed, accused everyone of callousness." I enfolded his hand in both of mine. "Including me. I was just as cavalier as they were about Mrs. Hooper's death."

"No," Nicholas said firmly. "They would've let her killer go free. You alone were willing to pursue the culprit. You wanted to bring the murderer to justice, if for no other reason than to prove Kit's innocence."

"Won't be easy," I murmured, "bringing a homicidal flowerpot to justice."

A wan smile touched Nicholas's lips, and the faintest hint of a twinkle lit his troubled eyes.

"I'd vote to pin a medal on it," he said.

I returned his smile. "Me, too. Mrs. Hooper was a truly horrible woman."

"I've seldom encountered a more deserving victim," Nicholas agreed. His hand relaxed, and the tension seemed to leave his body as he leaned back against the sofa. "The scene-of-crime team slipped up with the flowerpot. They didn't find the evidence they needed until Mr. Barlow told them where to look for it."

"Why didn't you tell us about the flowerpot when you arrived tonight?" I asked.

"Aunt Lilian didn't want me to," said Nicholas. "She wanted the villagers to have a go at one another. She believed it was the only way to purge the secrets and lies that had been poisoning the village, and she was right. It wasn't enough for you and me to discover the truth. The villagers had to admit it to each other."

I curled up next to Nicholas and twined my arm in his. Thunder rumbled in the distance, but the brunt of the storm had passed. Rain pattered gently on the stone steps, and the room was filled with the comforting snap and hiss of the crackling fire.

"Nicholas," I said, "what happened with the medical board?"

He gazed blankly at the ceiling. "I'm on indefinite leave. I can't resume my duties until I've sorted things out."

"What are you going to do?" I asked.

"Go back to London," he said listlessly. "Speak with more counselors. Wait for the board to declare me fit for duty."

My mind rebelled at the thought of his returning to an empty apartment. Three months of professional counseling hadn't helped him to cope with the trauma of his partner's death. He needed a healing circle of loving friends. I pressed my cheek to his shoulder, tightened my hold on his arm, felt his firm bicep, and was struck by a scathingly brilliant idea.

"How are you at digging ditches?" I asked, and without giving him a chance to speak, sat back on my heels and told him about the new drainage system Kit was installing at Anscombe Manor.

"He could use your help," I said excitedly, "and Emma has a million extra rooms she never uses. Stay with her and Derek. Work with Kit. I'll bring the twins to see you, and I know for a fact that you can have a kitten."

Nicholas was nearly blinded by the blaze of my enthusiasm, but after a moment's hesitation, he looked thoughtful.

"It might be good to get away from London for a while," he allowed, "but —"

"There are no buts," I insisted.

"But," he reiterated, "I doubt that your

husband will want me as a neighbor."

"Why don't you ask her husband?"

My heart kerthumped at the sound of Bill's voice. I'd been so carried away by my plans for Nicholas that I hadn't heard the front door open or the sound of footsteps coming up the hallway.

"Bill," I whispered, and turned my head in time to see my husband fill the doorway.

He filled it admirably. When I'd first met Bill Willis, he'd been bearded, bespectacled, pale-faced, and as soft in the middle as a loaf of bread.

He'd changed a lot since then.

An accident with an exploding stove had cost him his beard and in the process revealed a face so ruggedly handsome that I refused to let him cover it up again. Recent surgery had corrected his vision, so glasses no longer masked his velvety brown eyes, and five years of bicycling from the cottage to his office on the square had completed the transformation. My formerly soft-bellied husband was now as lean as a cougar, and his skin had the ruddy glow that comes only from ample doses of fresh air and exercise.

"Bill?" I repeated, looking him up and down.

He was dressed in a black leather jacket, a black T-shirt, and black jeans that looked as if they'd been painted on. I'd never seen him wearing jeans, leather, or a black T-shirt. It was the exact opposite of his usual style. But I could get used to it.

"You look . . . amazing," I said.

He surveyed my shapeless tunic. "You look —"

"Like a sack of potatoes," I finished for him. "I know."

"I happen to be very fond of potatoes," he returned. As he strode into the room, I noted with astonishment that he was wearing black leather boots. "Nicholas Fox? I'm Bill Willis, Lori's husband."

"I'm pleased to meet you, Bill." Nicholas shook Bill's proffered hand, but when he began to get up, Bill motioned for him to stay where he was.

Bill stretched his hands out to the fire, then sat in the vicar's armchair and crossed his legs. I couldn't take my eyes off his boots.

"I hope you'll forgive me, Nicholas," he said, "but I made some inquiries about you while I was in London."

Nicholas met Bill's level gaze. "I would have done the same thing if a strange man was spending too much time with my wife."

"If I had to choose a man to spend time with my wife," said Bill, "it would probably be you. You've an impressive record, and your colleagues admire and respect you." Bill hesitated. "I . . . know what happened to your partner. I'm so sorry."

"So am I," Nicholas murmured.

"I overheard Lori's proposal," Bill continued. "I hope you'll consider it. I have no objection to it whatsoever."

"None?" Nicholas eyed him skeptically.

"None," said Bill. He cocked an ear toward the hallway. "I believe your aunt has returned."

Lilian Bunting bustled into the room, caught sight of Bill, and stopped short.

"G-good evening, Bill," she said, looking rapidly from him to Nicholas. "I didn't know you were back."

"I finished up in London sooner than I expected," he told her. "I hope your meeting went well."

"It was marvelous, in its way." Lilian came around the sofa to gaze anxiously at her nephew. "Nicky, are you unwell? You were terribly quiet this evening, and you left the schoolhouse so abruptly that I thought you might have been taken ill." She put her palm to his forehead, fussing over him as she must have done ever since he was the twins' age. "It was extremely foolish of you to leave without your coat."

"Bill," I said, and jutted my chin toward the front door.

"I'm afraid we must be going, Mrs. Bunting," he said, getting to his feet.

"Don't let me chase you away," said Lilian, and while Bill distracted her, I spoke with Nicholas.

"Will you be okay if we leave?" I asked.

"I'll be fine," he said. "And I will consider your proposal, Lori. Are you sure Emma won't mind?"

"I'm absolutely one hundred per cent positive," I said, and kissed him on the cheek. "Sleep well, my friend, and dream of drainage ditches."

Nicholas's sea-green eyes sparkled with tears. He pulled me close and held me tightly before letting me go. "Good night, Lori. I won't say good-bye just yet."

I had to wipe my own eyes as Bill and I left the vicarage, and it took me a while to find my voice. When we emerged from Saint George's Lane, Bill started for the Rover, but I pulled him over to stand before Crabtree Cottage. The red geraniums looked like splashes of blood against the rain-washed window.

"Did Nicholas tell you about his partner?" Bill asked.

"Yes," I said. "It nearly broke my heart." I

291

looked up at him and said earnestly, "Thank you for making him feel welcome."

Bill wrapped his arms around me. "Nicholas has been through hell," he said. "We can't let him go back to London until he's well again, and for that to happen, he'll need Kit and Emma and Will and Rob and you."

"And you," I said, clinging to my husband. "Nicholas needs all of us. *And* a kitten."

Bill laughed. "Most especially the kitten."

I rubbed my cheek against his leather jacket. "Did I happen to mention how much I like your new look?"

"Man does not live by tweed alone," Bill said, kissing the top of my head. "Shall we go home?"

"In a minute."

I turned my back on Crabtree Cottage and looked slowly around the square. The schoolhouse was dark, but lights were on in every other building. The extraordinary meeting of the Easter vigil committee might have ended, but the villagers would burn the midnight oil, reviewing its extraordinary findings.

Nicholas and I had set out to capture a killer and had caught instead grudges and sausages, massages and marijuana, blackmail and a long-lost child. We'd discovered that Mrs. Hooper hadn't poisoned Finch on her own — she'd had the villagers' full cooperation. Would they be more wary when the rumor mill went back into production? I doubted it. As Nicholas had said, wherever two or more are gathered . . .

Yet my neighbors had proven themselves to be far more tolerant than Mrs. Hooper could have guessed. If Dick Peacock was cutting costs with smuggled liquor, so be it. If George and Miranda were having an affair, good for them. If Miranda sprinkled a few pot plants in with her other herbs, well, she was a sort of doctor, wasn't she? And pot had its place in folk medicine.

Peggy's child was no one's business but hers, and everyone knew that Kit Smith was a saint. If Nell wanted to set her cap at Kit, that was okay with them, too. Nell had always had an old head on her shoulders, and she could do a lot worse.

The villagers hadn't shed a tear over Mrs. Hooper's death, but as Aunt Dimity had predicted, they'd protected one another. Like a true family, they bickered among themselves, but when push came to shove, they stood united. Sally Pyne and Miranda Morrow would never be the best of friends, but they didn't have to be, as long as they were good neighbors.

I leaned back against Bill and smiled. For all of its turbulent undercurrents, Finch was still a blessed backwater. I could think of no better place to call home.

Epilogue

Nicholas returned briefly to London, to collect his things and sublet his flat. He took the tower room at Anscombe Manor and was promptly adopted by a fleet-footed kitten he called Rumor. Nell's black lab took to him, too, and the two could be seen every morning, jogging to Finch and back.

Nicholas, Kit, and Lucca worked like navvies all summer, installing the new drainage system, repairing fences and outbuildings, and looking after the stables. Will and Rob demanded daily visits once they learned that Uncle Nicky and Uncle Kit loved mud as much as they did and that Uncle Lucca would let them swing on the paddock gate.

Nell came home at Easter and took about three seconds to figure out Emma's less than subtle scheme to offer Lucca in exchange for Kit. Lucca was willing — seldom has a young man been more willing — but Nell remained steadfast, though she toned down her protestations after a long and private talk with Nicholas.

Nicholas and I spent much of Easter week delivering gilded gingerbread for the Pyms. Ruth and Louise had been baking and decorating ever since we'd left their house, and although Mr. Barlow had repaired their "motor," there were far too many boxes for the sisters to handle.

The vicar began the Easter service with a special tribute to Sally Pyne's magnificently traditional floral display and concluded it by introducing Harry Mappin to the congregation. Peggy and Jasper Taxman watched proudly as Harry nodded to the parishioners, and only Nicholas and I seemed to notice the small brown monkey peeking out of his breast pocket.

Nicholas and Bill confounded everyone in Finch by establishing a close and lasting friendship. Our threesome has provided the villagers with ample gossip fodder, but we don't mind. Bill says it's the least we can do to repay our nosy neighbors for keeping an eye on me when my eye was wandering.

My eye hasn't stopped wandering, and Bill's drifts from time to time, but the bond between us is stronger than ever. If a true marriage recognizes human frailty — and thrives on a certain element of suspense — then ours is the truest marriage I know.

Aunt Dimity summed up the murder investigation by commenting that *Finch is surely the only place on earth where the crime of the century would be committed by a flowerpot.*

Which is, she added, *why we love it.*

Nicholas seems to agree with her. It's autumn now, and although he's grown strong in mind and spirit, he's shown no inclination to return to London. Bill and the boys are delighted. Uncle Nicky has become as much a part of our family as Kit. Will and Rob — with mud on their minds, no doubt — want him to stay forever.

As for me, I say a prayer of thanks every time I drive by Crabtree Cottage. Prunella Hooper had been a blight upon the village, but even blights have their uses. Her lies forced the villagers to tell the truth. Her death brought new life to my marriage. She was the devil incarnate, but without her, Nicholas might never have found his way out of hell. Her evil had given rise to an awful lot of good.

I'll never build a monument to Pruneface Hooper, but when I drive by Crabtree Cottage, I give thanks.

The Pym Sisters'
Gilded Gingerbread

Oven: 300 degrees Fahrenheit
Yield: 15 cookies

    1 cup dark brown sugar
    1/3 cup honey
    grated rind of one lemon
    6 tablespoons butter, diced
    2 cups unbleached flour
    1/2 teaspoon baking powder
    2 teaspoons ground ginger
    1 egg white, unbeaten
    edible gold leaf (available at craft stores)

Butter two baking sheets. Warm sugar, honey, and lemon rind slowly over low heat until sugar has dissolved. Simmer for five more minutes. Add butter to the hot pan. Stir until it melts. Remove from heat. Stir in flour, baking powder, and ginger. Mix to a fairly stiff dough and roll dough out thinly on a floured board. Cut to desired shape. Transfer cookies to baking sheets with a palette knife or spatula. Bake for 20 minutes. Place on wire rack to cool.

When cool, use unbeaten egg white as glue to attach edible gold leaf in desired pattern.